El Payaso took another slurp from the smoothie sample. He looked at Alexis and held her gaze. "Not bad," he said, "I'll have to stop by your stand for another." Alexis stared wide-eyed back at him. Then he asked Santiago, "You remember your promise?"

"Yes, sir."

"I want you to stay away from my daughter, all right? Maria Elena's back in town, but I want you to stay clear of her. You got that?"

"Yes, of course, sir."

"Okay," El Payaso said, standing up. "You guys can go," he said to Alexis and Santiago. "But I'll be watching you."

border town

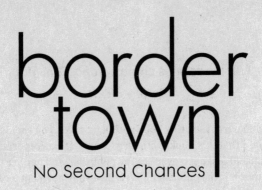

border town

No Second Chances

MALÍN ALEGRÍA

Point

To los primos chidos: *Nano, Panchito,*
Beto, y *Rickie*

ISBN 978-0-545-40243-9

Copyright © 2012 by Malín Alegría
All rights reserved. Published by Point, an imprint of
Scholastic Inc.
SCHOLASTIC, POINT, and associated logos are trademarks
and/or registered trademarks of Scholastic Inc.

12 11 10 9 8 7 6 5 4 3 2 1   12 13 14 15 16 17/0

Printed in the U.S.A.   23
First printing, November 2012

Caras vemos, corazones no sabemos.

Faces seen, hearts unknown.

chapter 1

Hello?" an excited female voice with a thick Mexican accent called through the Dos Rios High wall intercom. "Hello?" she repeated. "Is anyone there?"

A couple of kids in the back of the history class snickered. Sylvia Martinez, the school secretary, considered herself the eyes and ears of Dos Rios High School. Coach Cortez looked up at the wall speaker in annoyance and replied, "Yes, Mrs. Martinez. We can all hear you fine."

"Oh, good," she said with relief. "I'm looking for BJ Lopez. Is BJ in your class? His mommy is out here in the hallway and she has his lunch. She says he has a delicate stomach and that the cafeteria food gives him gas —"

"Mrs. Martinez," Coach Cortez interrupted. "BJ is not in this class."

Santiago started to laugh.

"So sorry," Mrs. Martinez replied before hanging up.

The teacher turned on Santiago with a heated stare. "And what's so funny, Reyes?"

"Nothing, sir," Santiago grumbled, sinking down at his desk. He held his tongue and tried to reread the paragraph in his opened text-book. Coach Cortez continued to peer from his large oak desk, daring Santiago to talk back.

Damn! This guy has no sense of humor, Santiago thought. He fought his urge to talk back, remembering his promise to his mother, La Virgen, and even to the trafficker Juan "El Payaso" Diamante: to be good. *Why can't Cortez just cut me some slack?* Santiago noticed that Cortez was scribbling something down on a piece of paper. *Is he filling out a referral for laughing?*

Suddenly, Mrs. Martinez' voice came back on the intercom. "Hello? Hello? Anyone there?"

Coach Cortez crumpled the paper in his hands, grumbling under his breath. "Yes, Mrs. Martinez?"

"Have you seen Santiago Reyes? The pretty boy with the curly hair."

The room erupted into hoots and applause. Santiago beamed, raising his arms in the air. He couldn't help it that everyone, but Cortez, liked him. The girl next to him smiled.

Mrs. Martinez lowered her voice to a whisper. "I think he's in trouble again. The assistant principal wants to see him and he did not look happy. They called in the guidance counselor and his *mamita*, Consuelo. You remember her, right? Didn't —"

"That is quite enough," Cortez said, cutting her short. "Settle down, class!" he hollered. Then he pointed to the door. "Go!"

[3]

"Sounds good to me," Santiago said under his breath as he collected his books. He gestured "*adiós*" to his classmates and exited the classroom.

The hallway was deserted. Santiago took in the silence, the wall of lockers, the posters for the upcoming school dance, and the scent of the citrus cleaner the janitor used year after year to mop the floors. He couldn't wait to be done with this place. If he could just keep his cool for a couple more months, he'd graduate onstage with all the other fools.

His footsteps echoed down the hall as he walked toward the assistant principal's office. He wondered what this meeting could be about. Maybe they found out who stuck those fake dollar bills to the ceiling of the girls' bathroom last fall. He snickered to himself, remembering how the girls screamed as they crashed into one another fighting to get the money. Or maybe they found out he was the one who took all the air out of the school bus tires at the Homecoming game. He'd pulled those pranks way before his promise. Those days — along with his drag racing — were over. They couldn't punish him for things he did last year, could they? Santiago's hands broke out in a sweat. Whatever it was, it couldn't be good, he thought, standing in front of the assistant principal's door. *Why did they have to bring in my mom?* He knocked.

"Enter," Assistant Principal Castillo said in an authoritative voice.

Santiago took a deep breath and opened the door. Castillo sat behind his enormous desk. On the wall were faded newspaper clippings of his former glory days as a high school football star mixed with affirmation posters he'd collected at statewide teacher conferences. Behind his desk there was a recent picture of the Mariachi Club. Santiago spotted his goofy smile in the third row, his accordion raised in the air.

Finally, Santiago noticed the other people

in the room. Two women sat across the desk from Castillo. They both turned around when Santiago entered. He immediately locked eyes with his mother. The pain on her face made him nervous. He wanted to run and deny everything. But his feet were stuck as if nailed to the floor. *The other woman must be the guidance counselor*, Santiago thought, taking in the heavy woman's '80s retro hairstyle and costume jewelry.

"Have a seat, son," Castillo said, gesturing to the empty chair between the two women.

Santiago couldn't help but flinch at the word "son." Castillo had been a thorn in his side ever since he started high school. He was always in his business and called his house with any excuse to speak to his mother. But the man wasn't all bad, Santiago reminded himself. Castillo had started that special program to help knuckleheads like him make up school credit; he became the advisor for the Mariachi Club; he'd even pushed Santiago to uncover a hidden gift for wooing the ladies with the accordion.

Santiago's mom, Consuelo, reached for his hand and squeezed it. Her pained expression alarmed him. Whatever he'd done, he'd make it up to her, he thought. He couldn't stand to disappoint her. It had been just the two of them since his dad left ten years ago. His mom was tall, slender, and had the face of an Aztec princess — the kind you saw on Mexican bakery calendars or lowrider magazines. She could have been somebody big like a TV anchor lady or a runway model.

The assistant principal cleared his throat and glanced at Consuelo. His mom looked down at her lap. What was going on? Santiago's heart raced and a thin film of sweat appeared on his upper lip. He quickly wiped it away.

"Santiago," Castillo said. The sound of the clock overhead ticked loudly, emphasizing each grueling second inching by. "I have some news about your father."

Santiago shot up in his chair. "What?"

"Consuelo just informed us that your father is out on parole. He wants to see you."

"No way!" Santiago shouted. He glared at his mother, begging for her to say it was just a joke. Consuelo held his gaze for a minute. That minute told him that his worst fears were true. "Oh, hell naw. That punk was supposed to be locked up for life."

"I was worried about how you would take this," Consuelo said, avoiding his eyes. "I think it might be good for you to see him. John" — she caught herself — "I mean Assistant Principal Castillo thought . . ."

Santiago tuned out the rest of his mom's sentence. John? When did he stop being Castillo? He looked from his mom to Castillo and to the counselor. This whole thing was like a bad case of *chorro*.

"Where are you going?" Castillo barked.

Santiago hadn't realized he had stood up.

Castillo's face softened. "Please sit back down. I know this news is shocking. It was shocking to me, too. Your dad and I used to be friends, did you know that?" His cheeks colored. "I guess what I'm trying to say is that you're not alone. If you ever want to talk —"

His mother cut in, "I hear you've been improving in your classes. He says you can graduate if you pass all your classes this semester. Imagine that" — her eyes sparkled — "my son, a Dos Rios High School graduate."

Santiago felt trapped in a snare. The thought of his father, a man he barely knew, coming back into his life was unbearable. Why did his mom have to come to school to tell him this in front of Castillo and the counselor lady? Was this some kind of intervention? Did she think he couldn't handle it? Their good intentions were suffocating him.

He remembered the last thing his dad sent him from jail. It was a belated homemade

SpongeBob birthday card. His old man didn't even have the decency to remember his actual birthday. Not to mention he thought Santiago was still a kid. In all the years his dad was locked up, Santiago had never once written or gone to visit him. Now, his dad was getting out and he wanted to see him. Did his mom want them to make up?

"I won't see him. We don't need him, Mom," Santiago said. "We can move someplace where he'll never find us, and I'll get a job."

"Santiago," his mother tried to interrupt.

"No, Mom," he insisted. "I'm not a little kid anymore. I'm not scared of him. I'll take care of you now."

Castillo cut in, "Santiago, don't misunderstand the situation. We all care about you and want you to stay focused on your education. Whether you see him or not is up to you. We just don't want you to be surprised if he pops up."

Santiago shook his head in confusion. His

eyes bounced around the room. These walls were keeping him back from what he really needed to do. The time for school games was over. He had to be out in the real world, making real money. Santiago had to protect his mother. The only way, the real way to do it was with money. He stood up and reached over the desk to shake Mr. Castillo's hand.

"Well, I want to thank you, Castillo, for taking the time to talk to me, hombre to hombre." The assistant principal looked surprised. Santiago smiled at his reaction. "I want to thank all of you for helping me realize what's really important." Then he turned to address his mother. He gave her a hug. Consuelo stiffened at his touch. "I don't want you to worry, Mom. I got this all under control."

Santiago took several steps toward the door.

"You've got fifteen minutes before lunch," Castillo pointed out, reaching into a drawer for his hall pass slips.

He waved Castillo's offer away with his hand. "Don't worry. I don't plan to go back to class."

The tension in the room began to build as the adults looked at him with confused expressions. Santiago couldn't help but laugh. They were all well-intentioned, but they were wasting their time on him.

"Where are you going?" his mother asked, the lines at the edge of her eyes creasing. She worried a lot about the mortgage and bills. He wanted to take all those worry lines away. "What about your books?" Consuelo motioned to the history textbook and notebooks he'd left on his chair.

He paused a moment. Their concern was touching. "Give them to somebody more worthy of your support. No, wait. Give them to the hungry children of Mexico, those kids who sell chiclets on the border. Yeah."

"Santiago." His mother's tone shifted from concern to irritation. "Get back here. What are you talking about?"

"I'm saying that I'm done playing the school-boy." Santiago raised his arms in a surrendering gesture. "This whole education thing I did because I made you a promise. But now my time is up. No more messing around. I'm going to get a job and I'm going to take care of you. I won't let him come near us. We'll go far away."

"Santiago." His mother stood up. "What are you talking about? We are not going anywhere. And I won't let you give up on your education." She looked at Castillo for help.

Santiago smiled. "I'm eighteen, Mom. I can do what I want. You can't make me stay in school." His mother flinched. He tried to make her understand. "At first I thought graduating would make you happy, but now, thanks to all of you, I see that what I need to do is be a man. I need to make money."

"That is ridiculous," Consuelo snapped, crossing her arms in protest. She raised a finger and turned her anger on Castillo. "John, this is all your fault. Do something."

Castillo cleared his throat loudly, obviously struggling for something to say.

"I know you don't believe me," Santiago interrupted. "You think I'm just a kid." His dad's birthday card flashed before his eyes. They all thought he was a kid. A rush of frustration gave him the courage to go on. "But I'll prove to you guys that I can do it." He opened the door. The adults in the room stared, dumbfounded. Santiago gave them one of his confident smiles. "You gotta trust me," he said. Then he walked out of the assistant principal's office and Dos Rios High School for good.

chapter 2

A small smile crept over Santiago's face. He'd been sitting in his truck in front of his uncle's restaurant thinking for the better part of the day, when it hit him. He could kick himself for not thinking of it sooner. Two doors down the street from his uncle's restaurant was a shady-looking storefront with paper on the windows and a homemade painted sign with the words *"Aquí Es"* that sold knockoff diet products like shakes, pills, and protein bars. People of all shapes and sizes exited the building carrying brown paper bags. He had counted ten customers in the past fifteen minutes. No matter how bad the economy was, people always wanted to be thin.

In comparison, only the mail carrier had entered his uncle's restaurant. Santiago wondered how his uncle's business was doing. Looking down the street of old downtown, he wondered about the owners of the vacant buildings lining the block. Starting a business was risky, but wasn't life all about taking risks?

Santiago hopped out of his truck and pushed open the restaurant's front door. A comforting whiff of bacon and beans greeted him along with the sounds of Tex-Mex accordion music. His uncle Leo's restaurant was a family institution. He grew up playing hide-and-seek under the tables with his cousins and stealing fresh flour tortillas off the hot *comal*. The walls were covered in memories — black-and-white photographs of his long-dead relatives in crazy stone-face poses, a colorful mural he had helped paint, and there was even a picture of him in his little-league oufit over the cash register. Soaking in his family's mementos, Santiago realized he came from a long line of merchants and do-it-yourself enthusiasts. He turned at the sound of his cousin complaining.

"But, Dad," Fabi cried, "it's not fair. How are local businesses supposed to compete? We should talk to the mayor. Or maybe we can change our menu a little, add some vegetarian options? That way we can be unique. No one around here does vegetarian Mexican. Dad, are you listening to me? Dad?"

Uncle Leo moved in a slow, careful manner behind the counter. His wide frame towered over his prep cook, Chuy, who was making circles around them, grabbing precut fajita vegetables from a refrigerated counter tray and dropping them over the carne asada grilling on the stove. His long black braid whipped back and forth as he worked. "Dad," Fabi said again. She frowned, crossing her arms in front of her chest. She took after her dad's side of the family, with her thick frame and almond-colored skin.

"Leave your *papá* alone!" *tía* Magda, her mother, yelled from the other side of the room. "Can't you see he's busy? Why do you want him to stress?"

"But, Mom" — Fabi turned to her mother — "it's not fair. How are we supposed to compete with 'Mr. Taco Man' opening up across the street? They're trying to run us out."

"*Hay mija,*" Magda said in an exasperated tone. "You and your crazy ideas."

"*Dios nos ayudará,*" Fabi's grandmother, whom everyone called "Abuelita Alpha," interrupted as she made the sign of the cross near her wrinkly face. Her thin pale fingers worked meticulously at a red beaded rosary. Alpha was dainty, just like her daughter *tía* Magda and Fabi's sister, Alexis. Santiago smiled. In his large family, everyone had an opinion about everything.

"God helps those who help themselves," Fabi countered. But her comment bounced right off her mother's shoulders like water on a hot grill. Her mother continued on with her duties managing the register as if Fabi hadn't said a word. Fabi shook her head and huffed in frustration. Her long brown ponytail shook back and forth like a palm tree in a storm. "I don't even know why I try," Fabi said in a loud voice as she started clearing a table of its plates and silverware.

Santiago hopped onto a stool at the counter right next to Grandpa Frank. He slapped the lean old man on the back.

"How's it going?"

Grandpa Frank's tanned face brightened into a big smile, revealing his gold tooth. "Well, I'm alive," he joked. "That's one good thing."

"I heard you dropped out of school," Alexis, his younger cousin, interrupted in a low voice from behind him. She seemed sweet and inno- cent, with her big eyes and easy smile, but the girl was too nosy for her own good. "Your mom was just here and she was *mad*." Alexis emphasized the last word in a teasing manner that reflected her true mischievous nature. Then her eyes became hard as stone. "When were you going to tell me about dropping out of school? What about the mariachi group? Do we mean nothing to you?" When Santiago didn't respond, Alexis narrowed her eyes at him. "Grandma Trini said you're bewitched. She and your mom went to find a brown chicken. I think they are going to try and exorcise the demons out of you."

"Ha! That's funny — and it's none of your business," Santiago said, shifting his body toward Frank. He gestured for her to go away. "Why don't you go get me some sweet tea or something?"

"Oh, c'mon," Alexis pleaded, pouting her glossy lips. "Everyone is talking about it at school. If you don't want to be in mariachi, that's fine with me — you weren't that good anyway. But I know they called you into the office." She leaned in and lowered her voice to a whisper. "What happened?"

Santiago knew he couldn't dodge Alexis. The girl would follow him incessantly until he told her what she wanted to know. "Fine. I'll tell you, but you have to swear that you won't tell anyone as long as you live."

Alexis's eyes widened as she mouthed the words "I promise."

"I'm pregnant," Santiago said in a grave voice. He sighed and began to rub his belly with a sad expression. "And the problem is I don't know who the father is . . ."

Grandpa Frank started to chuckle so hard his veterans cap almost fell off. Alexis glared at both of them. Then she punched Santiago on the shoulder.

"Ha ha," Alexis said in a taunting voice, giving him a fake smile. "Fine. Don't tell me. But don't call me when you are *actus reus*." She turned quickly, flicking his face with her shiny, straightened hair.

Santiago chuckled as Alexis stomped away. Ever since her mariachi boyfriend had been deported a couple of months ago, Alexis had started using big fancy words she'd picked up at the legal aid center where she volunteered. Now she was talking about being a lawyer. *Ha*, Santiago thought. That girl never picked up a book, unless she planned to throw it at someone.

He turned his attention back to Grandpa Frank. "Hey, do you still have all that food growing on your ranch?"

The old man studied him for a long second. "I've got some stuff," he finally answered, adjusting his cap. "Why?"

"I have a favor to ask."

"Does it have anything to do with this dropping-out business?"

Santiago winced, but he couldn't back

down. "Sort of. You see the thing is, I want to start my own business."

"What about school? A man needs to have an education."

"But you didn't finish high school," Santiago pointed out.

"I went into the Navy. It was a different time. You need a diploma to get in now."

"Uncle Leo started working in restaurants at fifteen," Santiago countered.

"Like I said, a different time. We didn't have the opportunities you have now. You don't want to break your back working like a *burro*."

"But school is just not for me," Santiago explained. "I want to work. I have this idea and I think I could make a lot of money, but I need some help. You and Fabi could be like my business partners —"

"My ears are ringing," his cousin Fabi said, coming up behind them. Santiago glanced over his shoulder at his cousin. Fabi held a bucket of dirty dishes against her hip and a firm frown on her face. "Whatever it is, I'm just not interested. I can't believe you dropped out, Santiago. You only have four months left —"

"Just hear me out," Santiago pleaded. "Hey, can you also fix me a plate? I'm starving."

"Get it yourself," Fabi complained as she headed to the sink to clear her bucket.

Santiago turned to Frank. "Who put a spur in her pants?"

"Didn't you notice that 'sold' sign across the street?"

He winced. "No, sorry."

"Some California franchise called Mr. Taco Man is setting up a whole bunch of taco shops throughout the Valley."

"So that's what Fabi was talking about! I love that place. I had like five of their Juicy Mex Mex Nacho floats in San Antonio. It's about time we got some cool spots around here." The look on Frank's face made him stop. "What?"

"Fabi is worried. She thinks we will lose customers."

"See, that's exactly why I want you and Fabi in my business. You guys know how to think. Having a good business is all about knowing your competition and looking for an angle."

"What are you plotting?" Fabi asked, serving a plate of steaming rice and beans with chili con carne in front of Santiago. She held out a fork for him and then pulled it out of his reach in a teasing manner. "You don't deserve all this service. Your mom is really worried."

Santiago leaned in. "Fabi, imagine having your own business. You can be your own boss. No one putting down your ideas. You can make up your own menu." Fabi squinted her eyes and folded her arms in front of her chest. She was waiting for the other *bota* to drop. "Just hear me out," Santiago continued. "You're always talking about wanting to make healthy vegetarian stuff, right? And Grandpa Frank, you got so many vegetables growing on that acre that you can't give them away." He paused and glanced at both of them. "Why don't we combine our interests and start our own food stand?"

Fabi's eyes widened. "Us?" Her eyes lit up for a second. But just as quick, the glimmer went out. She glanced over her shoulder toward the kitchen where her father was banging pots and pans together in a culinary massacre. "I can't leave my dad and mom alone. My dad is still weak from the heart attack."

Santiago noted her concern. "It wouldn't be like all the time. You could still work at the restaurant. We can have our thing on the weekends at *la pulga*."

Grandpa Frank raised his head when he heard the word '*pulga*.' *La pulga* was the weekend flea market where he used to sell his vegetables, hang out with his buddies, and make some extra money. It had been years since he had his little stand, and Santiago knew he missed talking to his neighbors and showing off his prized produce. Frank still grew the biggest heads of lettuce in town, but a lot of it went to waste. It was getting to be too much work for him.

Santiago turned to his cousin. "Look, Fabi, how much you make here?"

"I get tips," she replied flatly. Fabi glanced around the tables to see if anyone needed anything.

"Exactly. At that rate, you'll be an old cranky lady by the time you save enough money to travel like you want." Fabi nodded, so he continued. "And just think, we can split the profits three ways. I'll take fifty percent and you two get twenty-five —"

Fabi shook her head. "That makes no sense."

"Well, it was my idea."

"I don't care," Fabi protested.

Grandpa Frank laughed, slapping Santiago on the back. "I don't need any money, *mijo*. Your help around the ranch is payment enough for me."

"Great," Fabi said, all fired up. She reached out to shake Santiago's hand. "We'll go fifty-fifty, partner."

Santiago shrugged. This was probably the best deal he would get from his cousin. He shook her hand, sealing the deal. Fabi rushed away to serve a table of customers. Santiago smiled; a warm sensation filled his chest. The ball was finally rolling, he thought, digging into his plate of delicious food. Santiago would show his mom and Assistant Principal Castillo. He would show them that he was a man and he could take care of his family. More important, Santiago would show the man who called himself his father that he didn't need him.

"So you'll need to come by around five," Grandpa Frank said, interrupting Santiago's train of thought.

"Five p.m., no sweat," Santiago said, breaking off a piece of tortilla to clean his plate.

Grandpa Frank started to laugh. "That's a good one. I mean five a.m. You better sleep over. I'll let your mom know you'll be staying with me, so she doesn't worry."

Santiago shrugged. "Sure."

"Hey," Fabi said, stopping in front of him with several plates of piping hot food in her hands. "I was thinking veggie shish kebabs with this amazing homemade glaze. I made them once at a party and they were a total hit." She walked away before Santiago could tell her that he already had a menu in mind.

Santiago spun around on the stool to face the restaurant. Fabi was bustling around the room like a busy bee: clearing tables, seating new customers, and taking orders. Fabi was a hard worker who took few, if any, breaks. She was the perfect partner. He noticed Alexis watching him a couple of tables away. She had her schoolbooks out, but he could see it was just for show. Alexis was probably texting her friends from Mariachi Club or her boyfriend.

"Or maybe we can do something with cactus?" Fabi said, coming up behind him.

"I have a better idea. What does every woman really want?"

Fabi frowned.

"To be slim and sexy! Some men want that, too, of course. But we can be like those people on TV, selling the diet shakes, with those before-and-after pictures. You can be my model. We'll have to get you some baggier clothes. . . ."

"What do you mean?" Fabi asked.

"Well, we need a moneymaker. You know how people are all into that healthy stuff. If we blend slim, sexy, and organic . . . *bam!*" He clapped his hands together for emphasis. "We have a sure winner. You can take some before-and-after pictures. After you get all skinny, of course."

"Santiago," Fabi cried out and threw a dirty rag, the one she used to wipe spills and tables with. It hit him on the cheek.

"Fine." He raised his arms in a surrendering gesture. "You can be the after and we'll Photoshop some rolls —" Fabi punched him on the shoulder. Why were the women in his family so violent, he thought, rubbing his forearm. "I was just kidding. But seriously, Grandpa has tons of nutritious fruits and stuff. I was thinking we could run a juice bar? It's healthy, makes you slim, and tastes good. The best part is that customers don't have to do anything. No workouts. No giving up your favorite foods. They don't even have to chew." He pulled out a straw with the flourish of a magician. "They just suck."

"Maybe," Fabi said in a soft voice. By the look on her face, Santiago could tell she was letting the idea marinate in her head. Even though he had a couple of other ideas in the works, the juice bar was his five-star money-making plan.

The front door opened, triggering a bell chime. It was a couple of large professional women. He noticed that each of them held a brown paper bag, possibly from the *"Aquí Es"* store down the street. Santiago watched as Fabi handed them menus and took their orders.

His eyes lingered as they peered at the entire menu and turned it over as if they couldn't find what they were looking for. Fabi wrote down their orders and headed to the kitchen. On her way back, Santiago stopped her.

"Hey, what did they order?"

"They're sharing a chicken fajita order."

"I knew it!"

Fabi gave him a curious glance.

"Obviously, they wanted something healthy but small. Imagine their reaction when we offer small healthy meals in a cup." He shook his head in anticipation. "I'm telling you, Fabi, we could be rich."

Fabi stared. She wasn't quite sure what had gotten into her cousin. For as long as she could remember, Santiago was always planning get-rich-quick schemes. But she had to admit she liked the idea of having a business at *la pulga*. The flea market held many fond childhood memories: delicious food, cool stuff to buy, and a festival-like atmosphere. And she could definitely use the extra money. A small smile danced on her lips. She could have full control over the menu. Maybe if her dad saw that vegetarian dishes could be successful, he'd let her introduce new items to the restaurant. However, Santiago did have a knack for getting into trouble. But a small stand at the flea market sounded safe enough. What could go wrong?

chapter 3

Something shook Santiago's leg abruptly, jerking him out of a blissful dream filled with pretty girls, warm splashing water, and wet T-shirts. His eyes opened just a slit. It was dark outside. A rooster called out an early morning greeting. He rolled over, nestling back into the warm fluffy comforter, and tried to get back to his dream. His leg shook again.

"Let me sleep," he groaned.

"Not in my house," Abuelita Alpha said. Her gruff tone made his eyes spring wide open.

Suddenly, his blanket was yanked off his body. A burst of cold air struck him, making his arms and legs shiver with goose bumps. Santiago tried to retrieve the blanket, but it was gone, leaving him vulnerable to the elements. He curled his body into a ball and grabbed a couple of throw pillows to use for protection.

"Time to get up," snapped Alpha. She'd rolled the thick blanket in her arms like a burrito. "*Viejo*," Abuelita Alpha called out to her husband, Grandpa Frank. "See, now that's how you wake up the kid."

"Come on, Abuelita," Santiago begged, hoping for a little consideration. "Just five more minutes and I promise I'll be up." When Abuelita didn't respond, he smiled, snuggling deeper into the cushions of the couch. No woman could resist him when he asked nicely. It was one of his gifts. Santiago was surprised by how soft and comfortable the plastic-covered sofa was after a couple of hours of body heat pressed up against it. He wondered if he could find a way to bring custom-made plastic furniture covers back in style.

Suddenly, icy cold water splashed all over him. The shock made him leap up. Abuelita Alpha smiled. Her loose silver curls, pale wrinkly face, and oversized black clothes gave her an ominous appearance. The crazy lady had poured water all over her plastic-covered couch, converting his bed into a pool.

"*Mira*, Frank," Alpha said in a triumphant voice over her shoulder. "I told you I'd get that lazy boy up." She grinned at Santiago like she'd beat him in an arm-wrestling competition.

He raised his arms in a surrendering gesture. "All right! You win. I'm up."

"Don't make me do this again," Alpha said, reaching up and pinching him on the cheek. Santiago winced. Her fingers were cold but strong. "Frank is heading out back to milk the goats."

Santiago scooped up his red cotton T-shirt and denim jeans off the floor and hurried into the bathroom. A few minutes later, he was outside and ready to begin his brand-new business venture.

Grandpa Frank owned two houses. One was in town and the other, his ranch, consisted of several acres of land right outside the Dos Rios town limits. Only two acres were in production, the rest he left for the goats to run wild. When Santiago was small, he liked to come out to the ranch because Grandpa Frank would let him ride his donkey and hunt squirrels and quail out in the brush with his cousins. Other kids had their dads to take them camping and fishing. Santiago had Grandpa Frank.

The early morning air was warm and delightful. Santiago took a moment to scan the horizon. A shower of golden light from the morning sun illuminated everything in its path: the orchards, the berry bushes, and the rows of vegetable crops. He noticed lots of weeds all over the place. Grandpa Frank used to give him a quarter for every cluster of the thorny buffalo-bur he uprooted. It was a good deal for Santiago, until his cousins (his subcontracted labor force) protested getting paid five cents a bush and went directly to Grandpa Frank to cut him out of the deal. Santiago smiled at the memory.

A whining goat called out to Santiago. He turned and saw Grandpa Frank struggling with two pails of goat milk. Santiago rushed over and took the heavy buckets from the old man.

Grandpa Frank smiled. "Did she get you?" he asked, trying to stifle a chuckle. Santiago shivered at the memory of the bucket shower and Grandpa Frank laughed. "She would do that to me, too, you know? At first I thought to myself, *híjole* what did I marry?" He smiled brightly for a beat and then shrugged. "But if you marry a country girl, you learn to get up before her to avoid her temper." Grandpa Frank gestured toward the house. "Go set these on the kitchen table. Maybe she'll make us some fresh cheese." He winked.

When Santiago returned, Frank was feeding the chickens. The two then went on a tour of the ranch. Santiago followed Grandpa Frank down a row of leafy greens, carrots, cabbage, and celery. He listened to the list of chores for the day. There were weeds that needed to be cleared, the hen coop had to be refitted with new chicken wire, and there were tons of pests to trap, squish, and remove. Santiago's eyes glazed over as Grandpa Frank went on and on. He wondered if he'd bitten off more than he could chew.

It was past ten o'clock when Santiago started on weed patrol. With a garden fork and a rusty wheelbarrow he dug out the prickly burs and bindweeds that threatened to overtake the garden beds. Grandpa Frank complained about the sun and found a shady tree to rest under. Santiago looked down his first row. It seemed a lot longer than it did a moment ago. He wondered if it was getting close to lunchtime.

Suddenly, his cell phone started to ring in his back pocket. Santiago wondered if it was his mom. He couldn't keep dodging her, but he also needed some time to show her he could be responsible. The caller ID said it was his cousin Chubs. *Cool*, he thought, pressing ANSWER.

"Yo man, *¿qué pasa?* Where you at, man?" his cousin yelled above the bumping hip-hop music and laughter in the background.

"I'm over here at Grandpa Frank's ranch," Santiago replied. "He's helping me out with this business I'm starting."

"Well, tell him you got *chorro* or something. I'm over here at Travis's place."

Santiago's muscles tensed at the mention of Travis Salinas. He and his brother, Brandon, used to be Santiago's buddies until a year ago. In the past, Santiago helped them sell stuff like jewelry, car radios, and other knickknacks. He never asked where they got the merchandise — he didn't want to know.

But then came the trailer park incident. The brothers asked him for a ride to see a friend. The Salinas brothers told him to wait around the corner of this trailer park that was popular with the winter Texans. Then he heard a woman cry out. There was a gunshot and all kinds of scared voices filled the air. When the brothers appeared with all kinds of computer equipment, Santiago wanted out. He refused to sell the merchandise or have anything else to do with them. He'd heard that they had stopped stealing and were now transporting goods from Mexico.

"Dude! Are you listening to me?" his cousin yelled, drawing Santiago back to the present. "I said I've got these two fine-looking ladies here that want to go for a ride. They've never been to La Villa so I offered to take them. We're just up the street from you. I could swing by —"

Santiago thought about all the work he had to do before Sunday's *pulga*. Through the phone he could hear female voices. Someone asked if he was coming. Santiago looked over his shoulder. Frank was passed out cold and snoring loudly. Maybe he could go and come back quickly?

"These girls are getting very impatient," Chubs pressed.

"Pick me up at the end of the street," he said, lowering his voice. Santiago placed his gardening tool into the wheelbarrow. "Whatever you do, don't honk." He hung up and pushed the cart over to a mound of brush at the far end of the field. The blackberry bushes hid him from view so he ducked down and hurried over to hop the fence.

He got to the end of the block just as a midnight-blue Mustang appeared over the horizon. Chubs's head nodded to the beats banging from his car stereo. Next to him sat a pretty redhead in a cheerleading uniform. A blonde, in a similar uniform, smiled shyly from the backseat. Santiago loved blondes — even the fake ones.

"I want you to meet my cousin Santiago," Chubs said as Santiago jumped in the backseat. The girls giggled in approval. As Santiago relaxed into the backseat a sharp pointy object poked him in the back. He shifted his weight to find a jackrabbit with antlers behind him. Chubs was an amateur taxidermist — emphasis on amateur. Every Christmas, he gave the family a stuffed animal. Sometimes it was a dog or cat he found splattered on the road. Sometimes he created his own Frankensteinlike creatures. Santiago tossed the animal on the car floor. Once Santiago was settled, Chubs slammed down on the accelerator and took off down the rocky dirt road.

Santiago put his arm around the blonde. He caught whiffs of cinnamon and honey in her hair. "And what's your name? Or can I just call you gorgeous?"

The girl squirmed with delight. "My name's

Aracely, but you can call me Shelly. All my friends do."

"Hey, bro," Chubs held out a beer. "You thirsty?"

Santiago reached for the can. He leaned back and smiled at the girl in his arm. That's when the reality of the situation hit him like Alpha's cold shower. What was he doing? Santiago looked at the can in his hand and again at the pretty girl, who was now playing with his hair. He'd been cruising with his cousin and cute girls for as far back as he could remember. Then an image of Grandpa Frank waking from his nap nagged at him. It made him wince with shame. What would Frank think when he found Santiago gone? He definitely wouldn't be surprised, Santiago thought. How many times had Santiago started projects and then dropped them when they got boring or too hard? Ouch! Too many to count. At this rate, he'd never be able to take care of his mom. But now things were different. If he failed now, his father might try and walk back into his life. He might even try to get back with his mom and do the family thing.

"Stop the car," Santiago said urgently.

"What?" his cousin asked. He shot him a confused glance in the rearview mirror.

"I said stop the car," Santiago repeated louder.

"Dude, what's your problem? All that farm work making you crazy?" Chubs glanced over his shoulder. He didn't like the determined look on Santiago's face. He pulled the car over.

Santiago turned to the girl next to him. "I'm sorry. It was nice to meet you, but I got to go." Then he climbed out of the car. "Sorry, cuz, but I got to get back."

Chubs flung open his door to chase after him. He raised his arms, confused. "What's wrong? You don't like the girls? We can find other ones."

"Hey!" the cheerleader in the front seat protested.

The sun was high overhead. It was so bright Santiago had to squint to see his cousin's face. Santiago put his hand on his cousin's shoulder in a reassuring manner. "Man, it has nothing to do with you or the girls. I just . . ." He glanced over his shoulder toward Grandpa Frank's ranch. "I just need to go back to the ranch. I got to finish this thing I started. You understand?"

"No," his cousin said. "I don't understand. We got two hot girls in the car that are ready to have some fun. And they come as a duo — you get me? If you leave, then they'll want to leave, too. You can't do this to me, bro."

Santiago hesitated, feeling some of his resolve weaken. "I can't. My pop is out of jail and I need to take care of my moms."

Chubs's face lit up at the mention of his uncle. "No way? Uncle Eddy is out? How come I'm always the last one to find out anything in this family?"

"Dude, he hurt my mom. He used to beat her bad."

"Naw." His cousin laughed in disbelief. "Your dad never meant to hurt your mom. He just gets a little crazy when he drinks."

"You weren't there," Santiago said between clenched teeth. The seriousness in Santiago's voice made his cousin stop. Santiago remembered the paralyzing fear he had as a kid. How he would cry himself to sleep under his bed, worrying if this time his dad would actually kill his mom. He remembered begging her not to take him back, to press charges, and run away. But she never did. His dad always promised to change and his mother always took him back. *Not this time*, Santiago thought. This time it would be different.

Chubs stared down the road and said in a low voice: "If it's money you need, I can help you out. Travis and Brandon have a sweet operation going now, none of that trailer park thievery anymore. I'm sure if I —"

"I want nothing to do with the Salinas brothers. They got lucky at the drag race."

Santiago had secretly hoped the Salinas brothers would get caught at the drag race drug bust a couple months back. But someone was looking out for them and all they got was a slap on the wrist. "Besides, those fools are still pissed about their Escalade getting all busted up at the races. You think they're going to forget about that and let me work with them again?"

Chubs shrugged. "Maybe we could explain things."

Santiago gestured for Chubs to give it up.

"Well, you've got options, man," Chubs reminded him. "You don't have to shovel crap if you don't want to." He laughed at his joke.

Santiago sighed. "I'd rather haul a mountain of crap than work for those fools."

"Fine," Chubs said, letting the argument go. He glanced back at his car. "You sure you can't ride around for a little bit?"

Santiago shook his head.

His cousin let out a deep sigh. "All right, bro." He gave Santiago a handshake. "Smell you later."

It took Santiago an hour to walk back to the ranch. The overpowering rays from the sun sucked up all of his energy. Grandpa Frank was no longer in his chair. Santiago glanced at the dark house. Had he left? Santiago turned on the hose by the side of the ranch-style house and drank greedily from it. Then he raised the nozzle over his head to spray cool water over his body. Nothing had ever felt so good, he thought. Then Santiago knocked at the door. There was no answer. Was Grandpa Frank mad? He knocked again.

Frank had once said: *Fool me once, shame on you. Fool me twice, shame on me.* Did Frank think he was trying to fool him? Santiago spat, not liking the taste the thought left in his mouth. He paced a moment in front of the door.

Now what was he supposed to do? He thought about his alternative, the Salinas brothers, and turned to face Grandpa Frank's field. He stared at the rows of crops, the orchards, and the wheelbarrow he'd left out. This was the worst time of day to work outside. But what alternative did he have? Santiago had to earn back Grandpa Frank's respect.

Several hours later, Grandpa Frank appeared, offering a burrito and a glass of ice-cold sweet tea. Santiago ripped into the meal. He hadn't realized how hungry he was until now. The old man smiled, nodding in approval. "Alpha bet me that you wouldn't last an hour. You did all right," Grandpa Frank said, examining Santiago's work on the chicken coop. "Tomorrow, I want you to clean out the goat pen. You don't mind hauling manure?"

Santiago took a big gulp from the iced tea. He couldn't help but laugh.

chapter 4

Sunday mornings were *pulga* days. Rain or shine, the Dos Rios Flea Market was open and ready for business. *La pulga* was built on the remains of an old drive-in theater. Where cars once parked to watch movies, now dilapidated wooden structures were organized into a maze of stands selling used and new products: clothes, plants, furniture, CDs, movies, makeup, chickens, puppies, toys, tools, purses, vegetables, and anything else you could imagine. It was a festive scene, with a Tex-Mex band housed in an open-air warehouse and a dance floor that at night became the ring for Mexican masked wrestling matches, *La Lucha Libre*. Almost every town in the valley had its own *pulga*. Some were bigger than others, but each had its own unique flare. The Dos Rios *pulga* was the biggest in the area, and the place where fortunes were just waiting to be made.

Santiago put his arm over Fabi's shoulder as they entered the outdoor marketplace. "This is our new kingdom," he declared with pride.

Fabi smiled back, soaking in the atmosphere. She inhaled deeply, taking in the familiar scent and sounds of *la pulga*. It had been a while since she visited. A family walked by her and brought back a flood of memories of how she and her own family would come out on weekends to eat, shop, dance, and visit with friends. But that was before she started to work at the family restaurant. Now everyone was always busy. They never did fun things as a family anymore. When she was little, it seemed like the rows of vendors went for days in each direction. The place seemed smaller now, a little more run-down, but it still had the bustling carnival-like vibe she remembered from her childhood.

Grandpa Frank grinned from ear to ear as he glanced at the crowd. There were families straight from church, moms pushing babies in strollers, couples walking hand in hand, groups of teens, even a stray dog. Grandpa Frank motioned for Fabi and Santiago to follow him down a row of stands. He greeted the vendors as he passed. "*Buenos días*" and "good morning" they said, switching back and forth between English and Spanish in customary Tex-Mex fashion.

Fabi stopped at a stand that sold snacks. Her eyes danced over the products for sale: pinwheel-shaped, lightly fried floured dough; Mexican candies in flavors like tamarind, guava, and mango; and mini rolled tortilla chips called *taquis* doused in lemon, salt, and chili powder. Fabi didn't know what to eat first. There was just so much to choose from. She settled on a pickle. *I love sour things*, she thought, biting into it and savoring the explosion of tart juices erupting in her mouth. Fabi looked up at the sound of her name. Grandpa Frank and Santiago were waving from down the aisle. She hurried to catch up.

As they continued down the row, Grandpa Frank stopped every now and then to chat and reconnect with old friends. Santiago huffed in annoyance every time they stopped, but they were in their grandpa's world. It was his stand and his food they were going to sell. They had to wait patiently as Grandpa Frank set the pace. He introduced them to Mrs. Pulido, the plant lady, who sold a wide variety of potted tropical flowers; a man called Rana, who sold old records and antique road signs; and Papo and his ancient mother Doña Fifi, who sold religious artifacts and Jesus paintings that opened and closed their eyes.

Finally, they reached the end of the row at

the far back corner of the flea market. Santiago walked over to a rickety old weathered stand with a chipped table. With a rush of excitement, he jumped onto the table. The frame creaked under the weight. There was a snap from one of the back legs that split and broke in two, tossing Santiago to the floor.

"What is wrong with you?" cried Grandpa Frank. He pulled off his cap and slapped Santiago with it.

"Whoa," Santiago said, jumping up. He slapped at his jeans to take the dust off. "Sorry, Gramps. I didn't know that the table was falling apart." He gave Fabi a sheepish grin. "So what do you think?"

Fabi reached out and touched the wooden frame. The wood was worn from years of baking in the hot sun and torrential monsoon showers. A prick from a loose splinter made her cry out. "Looks great," Fabi said, imagining what the place could be with a fresh coat of paint. She glanced around, noticing that no one was walking this way. "But what about the customers?"

"I already have an idea about that," Santiago answered, giving her a wink. "But first let me go get the stuff." Santiago disappeared down the row of stands, back to the entrance where he'd parked his truck. It was loaded with produce from Grandpa Frank's ranch and covered with a blue tarp.

Grandpa Frank grumbled about the broken table under his breath. Fabi helped him mend the leg with duct tape and move the table to the corner to prop it against the frame. A few minutes later, Santiago was backing his truck into their spot. Grandpa Frank pulled out his aluminum beach chair from the cab, opened it, and flopped down into it.

"Hey, old man," Santiago protested, "we're just getting started."

"You bet, *mijo*, *you're* just getting started. But not me, I'm tired." Grandpa Frank took off his cap and wiped his brow with his carefully folded red handkerchief. "You took two hours getting ready this morning. You're not going to sell anything at this rate. All the real shoppers are already packed up and gone home. Go get me my cooler, *mijo*. I'm thirsty."

Santiago sighed and looked over at Fabi. Then he handed Grandpa Frank his little red ice chest.

Fabi still hadn't seen a soul come their way. She was quivering with nerves. Her dad didn't like the idea of her working with her cousin. He had warned her against it. But Fabi needed the money to travel the world like she'd always dreamed. She also wanted to prove to her dad that healthy food like juice smoothies could be profitable and delicious.

"So what's your plan to attract customers?" Fabi asked, taking a crate of baby purple carrots from him. Her grandfather liked to buy rare heirloom seeds for unusual things like purple carrots. Fabi was hoping the unique vegetables would draw customers' curiosity. She turned, looking for her cousin. He was on his phone, probably talking to some girl. "Santiago!" Fabi called out, trying to get his attention and motioning him to get back to work.

He nodded, hanging up his phone.

"Customers?" Fabi asked, feeling her temper rise. Her cousin never seemed to take anything seriously. "How are we going to get people over here?"

A shaking motion from the back of the truck made them both stop and stare. "I can help!" a familiar voice shouted, causing Santiago to fall back into a crate of celery. Fabi screamed out as her little sister, Alexis, jumped from behind a crate of navel oranges and threw her arms in the air with a dramatic flare.

"Damn, girl," Santiago cried, grabbing his chest. "You got to stop doing that."

Alexis smiled and hugged herself. They were both remembering the last time Alexis hid in Santiago's truck and surprised him. That time she had discovered his involvement in illegal drag racing.

"I'm sorry," Alexis explained, "but you left me with no other option. You didn't want to include me in your little scheme, so I was forced to include myself. Ha!" Alexis turned to her frowning sister and smiled. "If you want to attract customers, I'm your girl."

Fabi crossed her arms. "I'm not sharing my earnings. I always have to share. Not this time."

"Well, I'm not, either," Santiago said. "I didn't invite her."

"It's okay," Alexis said, wrapping her arms around her torso and swinging side to side. "I'm not interested in your money. I just want to be a part of whatever you're doing."

Fabi and Santiago glanced at each other. He shrugged. Fabi couldn't help but think back to her dad's warning. But it was too late, because then Alexis jumped off the truck and into her sister's arms.

"Oh, thank you, thank you, thank you," Alexis cried into her shoulder. She then turned to Santiago and gave him a hug, too. "You guys won't regret it. This will be so much fun. You'll see."

The three began setting up their stand. Grandpa Frank interrupted every five minutes to tell them where to set which vegetables or how to place it so it would look bountiful. Fabi grew frustrated with his indecisive product placements and started to make some sample spinach, aloe vera, and grapefruit smoothies. She had been experimenting with new, interesting flavors, hoping to wow the clientele. Her smoothies were not only organic, but they were local and seasonal. She smiled, despite the fact that her tongue was numb from testing out so many different flavor mixtures the night before.

Santiago's grand plan was to provide samples free of charge. Alexis and Santiago's job was to lure customers back to the stand. Fabi watched as they each filled a tray and then hurried over to the busier sections of the flea market. A horrible thought gripped her. What if no one liked her drinks? She should have had Alexis and Santiago test them out first. But it was too late now. Fabi glanced at her grandpa. He had fallen asleep with a can of beer wrapped in a paper bag in his cup holder, his mouth wide open. This was certainly not a pretty sight to attract customers.

"We'll have two orders of whatever you've got," a familiar voice called out behind her. It was her grandma Trini and aunt Consuelo. They were both wearing pretty dresses, having just arrived from church. Fabi noticed that their high heels were covered with dirt, but neither one seemed to mind.

"My first customers," Fabi said, beaming. She began mixing ingredients. It was a blend of cabbage, celery, and cactus, with a squeeze of navel orange. She served the brownish green blend in large cups. Grandma Trini reached for her wallet.

"It's on the house," Fabi said, motioning for her to put her money away.

Grandma Trini frowned. "How are you going to make any money if you keep giving these away?"

"She's right," her aunt Consuelo said, reaching into her purse and pulling out a five-dollar bill. She dropped it in the tip jar and smiled.

Fabi shrugged and waited to see their expressions when they tried the drink. The two women glanced at each other uneasily. Grandma Trini took a big gulp of the drink as Consuelo sipped slowly from the straw. Suddenly, Trini's eyes jerked wide open. Her cheeks blew up like a balloon and she spat the drink out dramatically.

"Grandma!" Fabi cried. "Are you all right?"

Trini coughed loudly, waking Grandpa Frank. The old woman reached for her daughter's hand for balance. Then she turned to Fabi.

"Honey, what was that?"

"The cactus is supposed to be good for your diabetes. It said so on the Internet," Fabi said with a soft voice.

"Yuck! My tongue feels all furry, like I've been licking a dirty lawn."

"Oh, come on," Consuelo teased, taking another sip, and wincing. "It's not that bad." She turned to Fabi, "It's an acquired taste, but it doesn't taste like grass, not really."

"Put some sugar in that," her grandma scolded. "Nobody will drink it if it tastes like medicine."

"It's supposed to be a local healthy drink," Fabi tried to explain. "I can only use things grown on Grandpa Frank's ranch, nothing else."

"That's rabbit food," Trini said, turning her nose up in the air. "I'm a human being. I need human being food."

Fabi sighed, rolling her eyes. Her aunt reached out and squeezed Fabi's hand in a comforting gesture. Fabi mouthed the words "thank you" to her as her grandmother continued to spit the taste from her mouth.

"I think what Fabi and Santiago are doing is commendable. They're trying to get people to eat healthier. There's nothing wrong with that," Consuelo said. "Where is Santiago?" she continued, switching topics.

"He's out drumming up business," Fabi said, motioning out toward the other stands. "He's giving out samples."

Grandma Trini's face went pale. "You're giving out free samples of that stuff?" she asked, gesturing toward the green goo in the blender. Trini swallowed and forced a tight smile on her face as she patted Fabi on the arm. "You stay in school, *mija*. Stay in school, okay?"

Fabi nodded. Dread began filling up her insides. What if other people reacted like her grandmother just did?

Consuelo pulled Trini away. "We're going to go find him."

"And I need some mint gum," Trini declared.

"Good luck kids," Consuelo said, waving good-bye.

Fabi watched them walk down the aisle and disappear around the corner. She tried to dismiss her grandmother's comment. Grandma Trini only ate sweet things — and bacon.

Fabi gathered the food scraps and tossed them in a bucket under the table. Then she turned over an empty crate and sat down. The day was getting warmer with each passing second. She made herself a smoothie. The green goo looked odd, but it was quite yummy to her. The hands on her watch ticked by with no sign of a customer. Grandpa Frank woke up and started to eat some of the purple carrots. She scolded him to leave some for the smoothies. Fabi glanced at her watch again. Alexis and Santiago had been gone for over twenty minutes. How long did it take to give away free samples? Then a thought made her sit up. What if everyone was gagging over her drink and that's why they still had no customers?

"I'll have one of everything," a voice ordered, surprising her.

Fabi turned and smiled into the soft hazel eyes of a dark-haired boy her age. He had white earbuds hanging from his big ears. It was her best friend, Hermilo, who went by his stage name, DJ Milo.

He smiled sheepishly and leaned over the table to get a good look at the ingredients. "So . . . what's the special?"

"Well," Fabi said in her best TV-game-show-hostess voice. "You'll want to try my latest creation." She followed his gaze to the green glob at the bottom of the blender. "You don't want that. You want an Onionlicious Carrot Dream," she said, nodding her head suggestively. "It may not look pretty, but I swear the flavors will melt in your mouth like the nectar of the gods."

Milo rubbed his hands eagerly. "All right, sounds good to me."

"Coming right up," Fabi said, raising her index finger in the air. She turned around to grab the carrots she'd put out a moment ago. Her heart sank. Fabi searched around and under the now empty basket. "Grandpa, I told you not to eat all the carrots."

"I didn't," Grandpa Frank swore, getting up from his chair. He helped her search for the carrots.

"Well, somebody had to," Fabi complained. "The carrots didn't just walk away."

"I swear, *mija*," her grandpa said in a serious tone. "I only had one."

"It's okay," Milo said, gesturing for her to forget about it. "I'll have whatever is left in that blender." He gestured toward Grandma Trini's "lawn juice."

"It's kind of an acquired taste," she warned, thinking of her aunt's comment.

Milo just shrugged. "That's cool. I like to try new things." He took a sip and his eyes opened wide with shock, but he didn't say anything. It took him a moment to regain his composure. Milo stuck out his tongue a few times as if he had to air the taste from his mouth. "Well, I should go. I'm looking for some old records. I just came by to show my support."

"How bad is it?" Fabi asked reluctantly.

"Not too bad. It could use some sugar."

Fabi winced. Was it really bad? She dipped her finger into the blender to taste the mix. It tasted kind of like pickle juice. Milo waved good-bye and disappeared down the row with his drink. Her grandfather elbowed her lightly.

"Good-looking boy, huh?"

"Grandpa!" Fabi cried out in shock. "That's gross. Milo is my friend!"

"I'm sorry. I didn't know you were so touchy about your friends," he said defensively. "I was just making conversation."

Fabi crossed her arms in front of her chest. Frank glanced sideways and noticed a small smile creeping onto her face.

chapter 5

Hey, beautiful," Santiago called out to a slender brunette with sapphire contacts. There were so many pretty girls at *la pulga* he didn't know where to begin, so he planted himself on a corner and talked to the girls as they passed by. "Did it hurt when you fell?"

The girl blushed as her eyes flickered back toward her group of girlfriends. Her friends encouraged her to talk to Santiago. The pretty girl shook her head, not understanding, and whispered, "What?"

Santiago licked his lips ever so softly. Girls

liked his lips. "Did it hurt when you fell from heaven?" he said. The girls giggled. "Would you like to —"

"There you are, *mi amor*," a girl interrupted. Santiago was so startled by the sight of Maria Elena that he almost dropped the platter of smoothies. Maria Elena, his ex and the beloved daughter of known smuggler Juan "El Payaso" Diamante. After he'd been caught in her bedroom in nothing but his shorts, El Payaso had shipped her off to Mexico and warned Santiago to never speak to her again. But now, here she was, in the flesh. Maria Elena smiled seductively at him. "Surprise. I'm back." She gave one look at the girls with Santiago, and they disappeared back into the crowd.

"Wow." Santiago laughed nervously. "You're really here. What happened to Mexico?"

"I'm back. I missed you, baby boo." She gave him a peck on the cheek. "I missed you so, so much. Did you miss me?"

"Uh . . . yeah . . . course I missed you."

Maria Elena glanced over her shoulder, a concerned look in her eye. "I lied to my daddy and said I was over you." Santiago stared at her with a bewildered expression. "That was the only way he would let me come back," she explained. "But don't worry. I don't plan to ever leave your side again." Maria Elena turned to glance over her other shoulder. She was definitely worried about something. Were her father's men lurking close by? "I have to go now. But don't worry. I have a plan." She kissed his nose. "Oh, how I missed this nose and these cheeks. Okay, I really have to go now. I'll be back, though — don't worry." And just like that, Maria Elena disappeared back into the crowd. Santiago shook his head to clear his mind. *Did that really just happen?* he wondered.

On the other side of *la pulga*, Alexis was dealing with a different kind of problem. No one seemed to like the smoothie. The first few customers just sniffed and waved the drink away.

Alexis tried to offer a free sample to a man looking at leather belts. At first he accepted the cup politely. He took a sip, but then he tossed it to the ground. How rude! The worst part was that he wasn't the first person to do that. Alexis sighed and turned back the way she came. She was not going to waste any more time on a product that wasn't any good.

"Santiago," Alexis whispered when she found him. "Something is wrong with the smoothie."

Her cousin shot her an alarmed look. "What do you mean?"

"Did you try it?" she asked.

"Why?" He shrugged, walking up to two teenage girls standing by a table heaped with cosmetics. He shot the girls one of his winning smiles. "Would you like to try something I whipped up just for you two beauties? It has natural stuff in it to make your hair shine and your skin pimple-free. Not that you need it. You two are naturally gorgeous." The girls smiled as they accepted the samples. "If you like what you see," he continued, "come visit me at my stand around the corner. Ask for Santiago," he said, and then continued down the row.

Alexis stopped to watch the girls' reactions to the smoothie. They both grimaced at the taste but stared dreamily at Santiago's backside. Alexis grabbed a sample from her tray and downed it quickly. A mucuslike, bitter flavor jarred her taste buds. *Wow*, she thought, *that was strong.*

"Hey," Alexis said when she caught up to Santiago. "This stuff is nasty."

"Doesn't all healthy food taste nasty?"

Alexis tapped her finger to her lips as she thought out loud. "What we need is a way to show people that this stuff will make you better — like medicine."

"I'm miles ahead of you," Santiago answered, pulling out a flyer from his back pocket.

Alexis grabbed the paper and read the ad promoting an amateur wrestling series right here at *la pulga*. The two guys on the pamphlet wore capes and masks like superheroes. She shot him a confused look.

Santiago smiled. "Check this out. I was thinking of signing up."

"You?"

"Yeah, Chubs and me. He can be my opponent," Santiago said, raising his arms as if he were going to tackle her. "Just think — tons of people will be there. Chubs and I could wrestle a little so people can see how small and weak I am next to Chubs. Then . . ." He paused for effect. "You pass me an energy smoothie looking all fine and sexy in some little dress and I wrestle that fool down to the floor. *Bam!*" Santiago laughed, loving his plan.

Alexis shook her head. "You're not serious?"

"Totally. It'll be great. People will want to try the drink so it can make them strong and quick. Did you try it?"

"Yeah," Alexis said, puckering her lips at the memory.

"And how do you feel?"

Alexis had to think about it. "I don't know. Okay, I guess."

"Just okay?" he asked, in a leading tone that made Alexis snort with laughter.

"Okay, I feel great."

He nodded in approval. "Exactly. It tasted bad. And bad stuff is usually good for you."

Alexis couldn't follow his logic, but she agreed to go along with his plan because she wanted to see Santiago and Chubs in tights.

"Yoo-hoo," a familiar voice cried out behind them, making them both stiffen. Alexis and Santiago turned to see their grandma Trini and Santiago's mom, Consuelo, walking toward them.

"Damn," Santiago said, under his breath. Alexis couldn't help but smirk, but there was no time to enjoy her cousin squirming because their grandmother pounced on them, pinching both their cheeks.

"How's business going?" Trini asked.

"What a surprise!" Santiago said, reaching out to hug his mother. Alexis studied her cousin. He was acting too friendly. Santiago turned to hug his grandmother, attempting to pick her up off the floor. Trini laughed, slapping him playfully and then scolding him to let her go. "Everything is great. People really like our smoothies."

"They do?" Trini asked, surprised.

"Yeah, people keep asking for seconds, but I just send them off to the stand. Only one free sample, I say. I don't know why I didn't do this sooner. Lots of millionaires didn't go to school, you know?" He elbowed Alexis for support.

"Yeah," Alexis agreed. "Like um . . . Christina Aguilera . . . and George Foreman."

"That's good, *mijo*," Trini said, distracted. She looked at Consuelo and nodded for her to talk.

"I'm making your favorite for dinner tonight," Consuelo said, in an overly cheerful voice. Her tone alarmed Santiago. He sensed a trap.

"Well," Santiago began, "I got a lot of work to do now that I've got my own business, and Grandpa Frank has all these chores for me." His mother looked down, wounded. It weakened Santiago's resolve. "But I guess I could come by around six."

"Great," Consuelo said, her eyes brightening. "Then we'll see you tonight at six."

"Whose 'we'?" Santiago asked.

"We have to go," Grandma Trini said, hurrying Consuelo back down the way they came. Consuelo looked like she wanted to say more, but Grandma Trini had a way of overpowering the conversation.

"See you tonight," Consuelo said, waving.

Santiago and Alexis stared as the two women walked away, wondering what they were up to. But they didn't get a chance to talk, because suddenly two tall, burly men grabbed them by the arms and pulled them away.

Alexis and Santiago squirmed, trying to wiggle free. A guy with an eye patch and a ponytail warned them to be quiet if they valued their tongues. The tough guys led them through the maze of booths toward the center of the flea market. Santiago noticed the fat gold chains on the guy's neck and his expensive shoes. He swallowed hard, hoping that it was just some mix-up. The guy holding him led them to a shoe shine stand. There, an old man was kneeling on one leg and shining a fancy pair of custom black boots with bright yellow lightning bolts and red eagles on each side.

Slowly, Santiago raised his eyes, taking in the customer's black jeans, big scorpion belt buckle, and collared shirt, unbuttoned to reveal an unruly mess of chest hair tangled with gold chains.

"I'll have one of those," the man said in a heavy Spanish accent, gesturing for the tray of smoothie samples on the platter Santiago still clutched. Santiago recognized the man at once.

It was Juan "El Payaso" Diamante. Santiago's escort reached for a sample cup and passed it to El Payaso. Beads of sweat dripped down Santiago's face as the memory of their last encounter came back to him. He remembered jumping into El Payaso's bed by mistake, hiding in Maria Elena's closet, and getting chased by his angry dogs. It was not one of his better nights. Later, El Payaso made Santiago swear that he would be good, not mess around in school, and stay away from his dealings. Panic gripped Santiago suddenly: Was *la pulga* part of El Payaso's dealings?

El Payaso accepted the sample. He nodded at Alexis. "You're Frank Ibarra's granddaughter?"

Alexis nodded, too afraid to speak. There were rumors about El Payaso — ugly stories tying him to violence and trafficking on the other side of the border. But no one had the guts to ask if the stories were true.

"Frank Ibarra is my grandpa, too," Santiago said, trying to make his voice sound brave.

"We're just helping him sell his fruits and vegetables. We don't want any trouble."

El Payaso studied the green goo in the little cup. He slurped loudly, twitched, and then nodded approvingly at the drink. "I mean no disrespect, son," he said to Santiago. "I just want to make sure you understand the rules at *la pulga*. Everyone stays at their stands and there's no stealing customers from other areas. I got several complaints that two punk kids were scaring away customers with a foul-smelling drink."

"It's my fault," Alexis jumped in. "He didn't want to do it." She gestured at Santiago. "It's my first time selling at *la pulga* and I thought if people tried our smoothie they would want more and visit our stand."

El Payaso nodded. He seemed to accept Alexis's story. Then he turned to Santiago. "How's school going?"

"Fine, sir," Santiago said, glancing at Alexis. He started to break out in a cold sweat despite the warm weather. Did he know that Santiago had dropped out? Did he know that Maria Elena had come looking for him?

El Payaso took another slurp from the smoothie sample. He looked at Alexis and held her gaze. "Not bad," he said. "I'll have to stop by your stand for another." Alexis stared wide-eyed back at him. Then he asked Santiago, "You remember your promise?"

"Yes, sir."

"I want you to stay away from my daughter, all right? Maria Elena's back in town, but I want you to stay clear of her. You got that?"

"Yes, of course, sir."

"Okay," El Payaso said, standing up. He admired the shoe shiner's work and smiled. "You guys can go," he said to Alexis and Santiago. "But I'll be watching you."

chapter 6

Later that evening Santiago parked his truck down the block from his mother's whitewashed Spanish-style condo. He glanced at his watch. It was five after six. There were two cars parked in his mother's driveway. The red Dodge Ram truck he recognized as Assistant Principal Castillo's. The silver Corolla belonged to his mother. Santiago smirked. He could handle whatever parental intervention those two cooked up to get him back into school. As he headed toward the town house, he thought about what he would say to them. The business was already taking off. And after his upcoming wrestling match, customers would be pulling their hair out to get at his leafy mojo energy drink.

Santiago was so wrapped up in his fantasies he didn't hear a voice calling out to him. Suddenly, sharp fingernails clawed at his forearm. He winced and twisted in surprise.

"What the — ?" Santiago cried, shaking his arm free.

Maria Elena stared back at him with a nasty frown on her face. She had changed into a black-and-white ruffled dress that accentuated her curvy body and tanned skin. "Didn't you hear me calling after you?" she snapped, shaking her silky brown hair.

"I'm sorry. I guess I was daydreaming," he said, giving her an innocent smile.

"Daydreaming about who?" she demanded.

Santiago did a double take. What had happened to the sweet, innocent Maria Elena that he'd known?

Maria Elena punched him on the chest. "Who is she? It better not be that skank Nina or Yessica," she threatened, lifting up her fist again.

"Whoa!" Santiago motioned for her to calm down. "You need to chill out, *mamacita*. I was just thinking about my new smoothie stand business."

Maria Elena sighed with relief, her angry scowl shifting into a flirtatious smile. "Oh, baby." She kissed him on the lips. "I'm so happy to hear that. You don't know how worried I was." She continued kissing him as she explained. "There was this crazy tarot card reader in Monterrey. She said you were running around with other women. I told her she was crazy and that you loved only me."

Santiago's eyes widened in surprise. He had never said that he loved her or that she was his only lady. They'd only hung out a couple of times before her father sent her to Mexico. Their time together was so brief, he hadn't thought very much about it. Maria Elena was hot and Santiago did want to hang out with her. But he also wanted to hang out with other girls — especially other girls who didn't have El Payaso for a father. He held Maria Elena's wrists and pulled out of kissing range. She knitted her penciled-in eyebrows in confusion.

"Hey, mama," Santiago said in a sweet voice. "There's no reason to get all worked up. Listen, I think you're great, but this jealousy stuff is not my style. I'm kind of a loner, you know, like a wolf."

"What are you talking about?"

He sighed. "What I'm trying to say is that I'm not really a relationship type of guy. If that's what you want, cool. I hope you find that. But me, I need to be free." He began to flap his arms like a bird. "You feel me?" Santiago waited for his words to sink in. She'd get over it, he told himself.

Maria Elena gasped, raising her mani-cured nails to her mouth. "Oh, my god. The fortune-teller was right." Maria Elena blinked hard. Then her eyes rolled back and she began to convulse like she was possessed by some demon. Santiago turned to scream for help, but just as suddenly Maria Elena stopped. Her eyes were aflame as she looked up at the sky.

"Are you okay?" Santiago asked with real concern.

Maria Elena opened her mouth to reply. "Here I was about to take you out for a night in Reynosa. Stupid me." The sound of her voice was menacing and sent shivers up his spine.

"Whoa, you scaring me, mama. You sure you're all right?" Santiago asked cautiously, taking a step toward her. Maria Elena stared past him, expressionless. She looked better, he thought. "Well, I just wanted to explain things to you. You know? So no one gets hurt." He moved in to hug her, but she blocked him with her hand and pushed him away. "Hey, no need to get physical," he protested.

"You think that's physical?" she asked in a stiff voice. "You don't even know the half of it. You played with the wrong girl."

"I didn't play you," Santiago said, throwing his arms up in the air. "We were just hanging out."

"Just hanging out!" Maria Elena screeched. The look on her face scared Santiago. It was time to end the conversation and get away from Maria Elena, he thought. El Payaso had warned him to stay away from her and he planned to do just that.

"I'm sorry," Santiago said, trying to sound calm. Maria Elena continued to cry: "Just hanging out!" over and over like a car alarm. He didn't know how to make her stop so he turned and walked swiftly to his mother's house. Santiago punched in the gate code, thankful for the security system, and rushed into the housing complex.

Pissing off a trafficker's daughter can't be good, he thought, pulling out his house keys. He wondered what Maria Elena, or worse, her father, would do next. At least he would be doing exactly what El Payaso wanted — he'd definitely be staying away from Maria Elena for good now.

"I'm home!" Santiago shouted, intentionally slamming the door behind him. He knew that Castillo and his mom had some thing, but he really did not want to walk into something that would take years of therapy to get over.

"We're in the kitchen," his mother called out in a singsong voice. Santiago hung his head as he walked down the creamy white hallway decorated with numerous portraits of him as a baby. His mom had framed every picture he had ever drawn and mounted them on all the walls of their home like trophies. It was pretty embarrassing, so he rarely had people over — especially girls. Animated voices were coming from the next room. Santiago paused at the entrance to crack his knuckles, then he walked in.

His mother was holding a liter of soda in one hand and smiling brightly at her guests. Her loose black hair shone like silk and Santiago thought she looked really classy in her fitted business suit. Castillo raised his glass for her to fill. His face was blotchy red and he was wiping his eyes like he'd been laughing a lot.

"What's going on?" Santiago asked, a tad annoyed at the situation. Weren't they supposed to be serious? Weren't they supposed to be trying to convince him to get his diploma?

The other guest finally turned and faced Santiago. The man looked familiar. He had short salt-and-pepper hair, a thin build, and a big toothy smile . . . that smile. Santiago glanced from his mom to Castillo, and back again in disbelief.

The man's grin widened. "What's up, Mini Me? You miss me?"

Santiago's insides twisted up into a tight ball. He felt his pulse begin to race. Santiago stared at the man who had brought so much pain and anguish to his family. What was his father doing here?

"What's the matter, Mini Me? *La Llorona* got your tongue?"

His uncles liked to tease him about how, when Santiago was a little boy, he swore his dad was the strongest, fastest, smartest man in the known universe. He'd seen the home videos where his four-year-old self imitated his dad's style of dress, his walk, and he even tried to talk like him for the camera. His dad thought it was cute and started calling him Mini Me. Now, hearing his old nickname made Santiago want to hurl.

"I like the big belt buckle." His dad gestured to Santiago's trademark belt around his waist. "You rockin' the cowboy look now? I've been out of the loop for so long. I was hoping the eighties would be back in style so I wouldn't have to go shopping." He laughed at his joke as if it was the funniest thing ever.

"What's *he* doing here?" Santiago spat, ignoring his dad and talking only to his mom.

Consuelo put down the soda bottle and placed her hands on her hips. "He's your father and he wants to see you."

"Well, I don't want to see him," Santiago cried, throwing his arms into the air. "I'm out of here." He spun around and retraced his steps back toward the front door.

"Santiago," his mother called out, coming after him. She caught up to him in the hallway. "Honey, please," she said in a soft voice. Santiago couldn't raise his eyes to hers. "He's been gone awhile and he wants to talk. Can't you just give him a chance?"

"Give *him* a chance?" Santiago asked heatedly. "Mom, that man is not my father. He was never there for us. I don't know what he told you, but I'm sure it's all lies. And I can never forgive him for hitting you." His mother flinched.

"That was a long time ago," Consuelo said gravely. She looked up at Santiago with a slow-burning strength in her eyes. "And I have forgiven him." Santiago jumped back against the wall. Consuelo leaned back and crossed her arms in front of her chest. "Your father doesn't always make the right decisions, but he's not a bad person." She paused. "Do you know why your dad went away?"

"Because he's a no-good, lying drug dealer," Santiago spat.

"College."

Santiago shook his head in disbelief. "Mom, please, don't —"

"No," she interrupted. "You never wanted to hear before, but I want you to know that your father did what he did because we didn't have any money and I wanted to go to college. At the time, I didn't know what he was doing. He told me he found a good job and I believed him because I wanted to believe him. But then he got busted trying to sell to an undercover cop. I know it doesn't excuse what he did or how he treated me, but I wanted you to know the truth." Santiago shook his head in confusion. "I've put that part of my life behind me. I've forgiven him for lying and I've moved on." She reached out for his hand and held it firmly as she held his gaze. "You don't have to worry about me, son. I will never let anyone hurt me like that again. Do you understand? Eddy knows it's over between us. He knows what he did was wrong. The past is buried, but not forgotten. And I think that if you just gave him a chance —"

Santiago could see his mom's lips moving, but he couldn't listen anymore to her words. This information was blowing his mind. Anger flared through his bones but then, an overwhelming sense of sadness overtook him. "Why didn't you tell me?" He could hear his voice threatening to crack. "I thought we were close, you and me."

His mother smiled, her eyes tearing up. She gave him a heartfelt embrace. Consuelo sighed into his shoulder and he breathed in her floral shampoo. "I tried many times, but every time I brought him up you pushed me away." She pulled back to see his reaction. "When I learned that your father was getting out, I didn't know how to tell you. That's why I went to your school. . . ."

Suddenly, Santiago noticed how quiet the house had gotten. Where were Castillo and his father? The idea of those two listening in on this intimate moment made the hairs on the back of his neck stand up. "Mom, can we talk more about this later?" he asked, listening for any sound from the other room.

"Sure, honey," Consuelo said, giving him another squeeze. "We can talk after dinner."

"Aww, Mom," Santiago complained. "Do I really have to?"

"Don't be like that. The enchiladas are probably already cold. C'mon." She gestured, taking a few steps forward.

• • •

Dinner was unusually quiet. It was obvious that the guests had eavesdropped on his conversation. His mom tried to be polite and share the highlights of Santiago's life thus far. However, in the past ten years there were few proud moments to gush over. Castillo yapped on and on about the Mariachi Club. He said Santiago had a natural gift with the accordion and talked about how much the group missed him. Eddy acted impressed and excited by the news. He tried to crack some jokes, but they fell flat.

"Hey, son," Eddy said, when his mom and Castillo started clearing plates. "I've got something for you."

His father opened his shirt to reveal a hand-sized tattoo picture of five-year-old Santiago on his left breast. Santiago didn't know how to feel about it. Usually guys tattooed animals or their girlfriends' names on their bodies. Seeing his face reflected back to him was weird. His mother came over for a better view.

"Oh, my," she said, glancing at Santiago's reaction and then back to the tattoo. "That looks just like him. Look, John." She gestured for Castillo to come over. Then she asked, "Did it hurt?"

Eddy sniffed as he buttoned up his shirt. "A little. No biggie. I wanted to do something for my boy," he said to Consuelo, but not taking his eyes off Santiago.

"Thanks, I guess." Santiago shrugged, looking down. "Can I be excused now? I have a lot of work to do tomorrow at Grandpa Frank's."

His mother looked disappointed. "I was hoping you'd stay awhile. I made your bed," she added in a light voice. "We can talk about your plans. . . ."

"I really should get back," Santiago said, getting up. "We're getting bees delivered tomorrow. Grandpa Frank says honey might make our smoothies a little easier to swallow." He grinned.

His father slapped him on the back forcefully. "That's my boy. Entrepreneur, just like his old man."

Santiago jerked away from him. "I'm nothing like you."

"I'm sorry," Eddy said, shame washing over his face. "I didn't mean —" He swallowed the rest of his statement.

"I'm out of here. Thanks for dinner. I'll see you, Castillo," Santiago said, ignoring his father on purpose. He hurried out the door and down a flight of stairs, pausing slightly at the front gate to make sure Maria Elena was not waiting for him in the bushes. The coast was clear, but his truck wasn't. Jagged letters were keyed across the driver's door and the hood of the truck. The words "liar" and "cheater" stared back at him. Santiago stomped the ground and cursed in frustration.

"Yo, son, wait up," a voice called to him.

Santiago's back muscles stiffened, but there was no place to run.

Eddy smiled when he approached. "I'm sorry about tonight. I guess I was just kind of nervous, you know, seeing your mom and John after so many years." He rolled his eyes. "Talk about a humorless bunch. I thought I was going to drown in boredom back there. Whoa," he said, seeing the words carved into Santiago's truck. "You having girlfriend problems?"

"What do you want?" Santiago asked, annoyed.

"Hey, I have a buddy who can fix that up for you real cheap. It'd be fun. You and me hanging out like old times. You used to cry whenever I left the house. You remember that?"

"That was a long time ago," Santiago said, glaring past his father down the street. "Thanks, but no thanks."

Eddy started to rub his hands together, as

if he were cold, despite the warm evening. "How 'bout we grab some coffee?"

"Coffee?"

His father blushed and pulled something out of his pocket. He handed it to Santiago. It was a yellow plastic chip, like the ones Grandma Trini got at the underground gambling dens she liked to frequent after church. "I've been sober ten years come September."

Santiago squeezed the chip, trying to break it in two. "That's not hard to do when you're locked up," he snapped. "Why are you really here?" Santiago asked, pinning his dad with his gaze.

Eddy lowered his eyes and shoved his hands in his pockets. "I came to see you."

"We don't need you."

Eddy gave a nervous chuckle. "I can see that." He looked over his shoulder at the complex. "Looks like your mom's doing all right all by herself."

"She is. We both are." A pang of guilt stabbed him. Even though his mom dressed nicely and they had the condo, Santiago knew they were living paycheck to paycheck. His mother had borrowed money last month to pay the mortgage. But it was none of his father's business.

His father's face softened. "C'mon, son. I'm your father. Give me another chance."

"No," Santiago said, his voice cold as ice. "You're not my dad. You quit being my dad the day you raised a fist to my mom's face." He opened his truck door and stopped. "You know the day they took you away?" His father nodded. "That was the happiest day of my life," Santiago said. He jumped into his truck and drove down the street.

chapter 7

A week later, Santiago's truck looked like it had been in a fight. Silver tape concealed Maria Elena's parting words like Band-Aids. When Santiago made his fortune, he promised himself the most expensive paint job ever. He took a calming breath. There was a lot riding on this evening.

It was the night of the wrestling match and Santiago had stopped at his *tío*'s restaurant to borrow some olive oil. He thought about how the oil would make his body glisten. It would drive the ladies in the audience wild. As he grinned, two men in heavy coats and dark hats walked in front of his truck toward the Mr. Taco Man shop.

Santiago took a moment to admire the new fast-food joint. His eyes widened at the grand opening promotion hanging loosely off the cartoon Taco Man mascot. *Four tacos for a dollar! What a deal*, Santiago thought. Then his eyes darted back to the curiously dressed pair. Something about those two bothered him. Was it the thick winter coats this time of year? Or how they stared into the windows like hungry kids? Santiago couldn't shake an uneasy feeling. He didn't like strangers poking around his community.

Santiago walked right up to the man in the wide-brim bucket hat and tapped him on the shoulder. "Can I help you?" he asked. The stranger jumped back into the light, revealing a familiar face behind a pair of dark Locs sunglasses and a penciled-in goatee. "Fabi!" Santiago cried in surprise. Then he turned to her partner and swiped the beret off his head. It was her best friend, DJ Milo. Santiago looked around for Alexis; she was never too far away. But Alexis was nowhere to be found. He turned back to Fabi. "What are you two doing? And where's your sister?"

Fabi shushed him and gestured for him to follow her into the doorway of a neighboring building. Then she glanced up and down the block. When Fabi was sure no one would sneak up on them, she leaned in and whispered: "We're infiltrating the enemy."

Santiago busted up laughing, "Who? Mr. Taco Man?" He looked to Milo for confirmation. *Poor dude*, Santiago thought, taking in Milo's long coat and furry collar. Milo was so in love with his cousin he would go along with any harebrained idea she had. It was obvious to everyone but Fabi.

"Your cousin wanted to see who exactly was eating in there and what they were order-ing," Milo explained, pulling off his oversized women's sunglasses. "Then we were going to sneak into the kitchen to find out the recipe for Mr. Taco Man's secret sauce."

Santiago pressed his lips together to hold back a chuckle. His cousin was harmless, but this was not the time to encourage her crazy activities. He had to find Alexis. "Fabi, don't you remember? Tonight's my wrestling match. I need you and your sister to be there. Alexis is supposed to be my Leafy Valley Mojo girl."

Fabi glanced at her watch. "Alexis took off about twenty minutes ago with her friend Justin. She said she had mariachi rehearsal."

"Practice? On a Saturday night?" he asked in a skeptical voice. Santiago used to be in the Mariachi Club at school. He was pretty good, too. But they'd never practiced on a Saturday night when he was in it. Santiago grabbed Fabi's elbow and pulled her toward his truck. "Well, then you'll have to fill in for her."

"Whoa," Fabi protested, pulling away from

him. "What about my mission? My parents won't admit it, but I know they're worried about losing customers to Mr. Taco Man. If I can just find out who's in there —"

Santiago released her. "Fabi, I don't get why Mr. Taco Man means so much to you. Restaurants open and close all the time. The smoothie shop is *our* thing. This wrestling match is going to get us tons of publicity. After tonight, people are going to be fighting to get their hands on our Leafy Valley Mojo. We're business partners, Fabi — and we're on the verge of something really big," Santiago pleaded. He glanced from Milo to Fabi, trying to read their reactions. "You're going to have to choose . . . Mr. Taco Man or me?"

Fabi glanced over Santiago's shoulder from her parents' old business to the shiny new neon-lit Mr. Taco Man. The idea of this fast-food bully coming into her town and stressing her parents out made her skin crawl. But Santiago was right. The smoothie stand was their business. "Fine," she said, surrendering. Mr. Taco Man would have to wait.

"Great!" Santiago clapped his hands together in a triumphant manner. "Can you go grab me a bottle of olive oil? It's for the show," Santiago explained. When Fabi returned, he motioned for Milo and Fabi to hop in his truck. "We better hurry. Chubs is already at *la pulga*." He glanced at Fabi's outfit and frowned. There was no way she could be his Leafy Valley Mojo girl dressed in men's clothes. "Do you mind changing into something sexier?"

"Santiago!" Fabi cried in horror. She looked at her face in the rearview mirror and smiled at the drawn-in goatee. With the sleeve of her coat she rubbed her face clean.

At night, *la pulga* looked ominous. The soft yellow glow from streetlamps cast gloomy shadows on empty stands and deserted pathways. It reminded Santiago of a scene from some horror movie. However, Santiago was not deterred and led Fabi and Milo down toward the wrestling ring. They could hear the audience roar from outside.

"Are you a real *luchador*?" a small voice asked, pulling on Santiago's shirt. He looked down at a little boy with short black hair and red Converse who had appeared from the shadows. The kid looked about eight years old, Santiago thought. He scanned the area, searching for the boy's parents.

"Do you want my autograph?" Santiago asked, leaning down to the boy's eye level.

"Only if you win," the boy answered and took off running ahead of them to the warehouse.

Santiago snorted, "Can you believe that kid?"

Fabi smirked. She was carrying a pitcher of freshly juiced Leafy Valley Mojo. Of all her cousin's schemes, this had to be the craziest one. She sighed loudly to no one in particular as she tugged down on the supertight red dress she'd borrowed from her *tía*.

Chubs greeted them at the doorway. He was dressed in a yellow bodysuit and black cape — like a bumblebee on steroids. Once inside, Fabi, Milo, and Santiago gasped at the enormity of the scene. A professional wrestling ring stood in the center of the warehouse under beams of harsh lights. Hopping around the mat were two shirtless middle-aged men in bright masks. A short balding man in a striped shirt was refereeing the match.

Santiago knew that although *Lucha Libre* was known for its colorfully masked fighters, high-flying maneuvers, and fancy holds, the rules were similar to American wrestling: pin your opponent to the mat for three counts and win the match. Santiago liked the masks. In some Mexican matches, the loser's mask was permanently removed and his head shaved. Santiago fingered his famous locks and was glad that this would just be a friendly game.

Lucha Libre was all about anonymity. However, in a town as small as Dos Rios, there was no such thing as anonymity. Santiago recognized City Council member Rey Garcia III and his old Sunday school teacher on the mat. As a kid, Santiago had liked to watch *Lucha Libre* on TV with his grandma Trini. His grandma called the *luchador* a people's hero. In the ring, every man was a fighter, no matter his class, education, or background. On the mat, every man was equal.

The little boy from outside slid up to Santiago. "I hear you're going to fight that big guy," he said, gesturing toward Chubs. Santiago smiled at Chubs's menacing bumblebee costume.

He leaned in to the boy's ear: "I have a secret potion that'll help me get real strong."

"You do?" The boy sounded impressed. Santiago winked.

Twenty minutes later, Santiago and Chubs stood in the center of the ring, bathed in a coat of olive oil, masked, and ready to begin.

Santiago raised his arms overhead, showing off his outfit. His purple pleather pants and matching sleeveless top looked great against his skin. To think he'd almost missed them, because they'd been misplaced in the women's fitness section! Santiago raised the lip of his silver mask — to let in some air — and took a moment to glance around at the audience.

There were people of all ages chatting boisterously in the lines of folding chairs set up around the ring. Children in brightly colored wrestling masks and even the hot dog vendor watched with enthusiasm. Santiago couldn't help but get caught up in the feverish energy of the arena.

Suddenly, Santiago spotted his dad standing alone at the back of the room. His mouth went dry. *Why can't he just leave me alone?* Annoyance flared up his spine. Santiago took a deep breath and tried to focus on all the potential customers. But then he noticed Juan "El Payaso" Diamante with his daughter, Maria

Elena, sitting in the VIP section of the room. Now, he definitely felt sick — he might even throw up.

From the right side of the arena, someone called out his name. He leaned over the rail to see a group of girls from his school cheering enthusiastically for him. Maria Elena also heard and she narrowed her eyes at him. *So much for anonymity*, Santiago thought. Behind him stood Fabi and Milo. In her trembling hands, Fabi held the pitcher with the magical elixir.

Chubs stared with a dazed expression from across the mat. His gold-colored mask and bathrobe couldn't hide his discomfort. Santiago gestured for him to take off the bathrobe. Chubs's eyes widened.

"Dude." Santiago hurried over and tugged at his cousin's robe. "You got to take this thing off." Chubs nodded, timidly removing his robe and hanging it over the rope. "Now remember," Santiago lowered his voice. "You have to make

it look real. I don't want you to hold back."
Chubs nodded, lowering his eyes. "Just do it
like how we used to wrestle when we were
kids," Santiago reminded him. "But remember,
after the second bell, I'll take a drink from the
Leafy Valley Mojo and you're gonna have to fall
KO style. I'll try not to hurt you." He shrugged.
"But I can't make any promises." Suddenly, the
bell interrupted him, announcing the start of
the match.

Santiago bobbed back and forth as he'd
seen *luchadores* do on TV. Chubs may be as big
as a refrigerator, but Santiago was quick. His
cousin made a move and lurched for him.
Santiago swiveled out of reach and raced to the
opposite side of the arena. Cheers erupted
from the crowd. Santiago turned and pounded
his chest like a gorilla as he yelled out his
wrestler name: El Puma. Then shouts for El
Puma filled the air and Santiago's heart swelled.
The cheers felt good, but he was supposed to
be losing. Santiago didn't have long to worry

about that, however, because a heavy weight crashed into him, knocking the wind out of his lungs.

It took Santiago a minute to realize what had happened. He was on his belly. The right side of his face was squashed down into the mat and he couldn't move his arms. All he could hear was the voice of the referee counting off. *No!* Santiago's eyes shot open. This was not how they had planned it. Santiago thrashed and squirmed under his cousin's enormous weight. "Get off me, you muck."

"Sorry," Chubs mumbled, rolling quickly to the right. *Whoa, that was close*, Santiago thought, eyeing Chubs angrily — too close. Santiago's heart was pounding and there were beads of sweat dripping down his shoulder blades. He glanced around, trying to orient himself. Out of the corner of his eye he saw Chubs rush toward him again like a swarm of yellow jackets. Santiago dodged him just in the nick of time. Santiago was going to crack a joke when a heavy hand grabbed his collar and tossed him back like a rag doll into the ropes. Santiago wanted to call a time-out, but the crowd was ablaze. People were out of their seats and crying out to him to fight back. He had them right where he wanted. If only he could keep his cousin from beating him to a pulp.

This was the moment to introduce the drink, he thought. Santiago glanced at the referee, willing him to call time. Chubs had other ideas, however, and tackled him to the mat. Santiago tried to pull himself up to no avail. Chubs was taking his part of the act a little too seriously.

Out of the corner of his eye, Santiago saw Fabi waving frantically to him from the sideline. She had a cup of the Leafy Valley Mojo in her hand with a straw dangling out. If only he could get his lips to the drink. Santiago tried to claw his way out from under Chubs and toward Fabi. But his cousin weighed a ton. Then the bell rang. It was the end of round one and Chubs sprang up and off his legs. Santiago rolled over and sighed with relief.

When he had regained a little strength, Santiago crawled over to Fabi. She was stammering about what a stupid idea this was. Milo had the sense to get a cold wet rag to help wipe the sweat from under Santiago's mask.

Santiago could barely keep his head up. He glanced over in Chubs's direction. Chubs was laughing with his head thrown back as some girls giggled in his ear. It took Santiago a full second to realize that those were the same girls who were supposed to be rooting for him. *What backstabbers!* he thought. Then he noticed El Payaso Diamante reach out to shake his cousin's hand. What's he doing? *Oh, no*, Santiago thought, feeling his insides knot up. El Payaso leaned in to Chubs's ear. He said something that made Chubs gasp in surprise. Chubs shot him a worried glance. Then to make matters worse, Maria Elena came up behind her dad and gave Chubs a kiss on the cheek. Maria

Elena glanced up at Santiago and mouthed the words "You're dead." He forced himself not to worry. He had no time to question what was going on. It was time to act — time to sell his product. He grabbed the elixir from Fabi's hands and turned to the audience.

"Ladies and gentlemen." The crowd hushed to listen. "Many of you may think this match is over. Some of you may have even placed bets against me. I know I am smaller than my opponent."

"You bet you are, honey," an ancient-looking woman called out from her walker right in the front row.

Santiago smiled at the crowd's reaction. "But what you don't know is that I have this new energy drink called Leafy Valley Mojo. My cousin and I sell it here at *la pulga* every Sunday. This drink will not only make you lose weight, but it will give you energy and virility — make you strong like a bull. The best part is that it's all natural — made with fruits and veggies only the Rio Grande Valley can provide. It's an old family secret and for $5.99 per cup, it can be yours."

"Stop jabbering and fight," a kid yelled in Spanish.

Santiago grinned confidently at the audience. Then he gulped back the elixir in one go. The concoction sent a shock up and down his body like a bright bolt of electricity. When Santiago recovered, he turned to his opponent and smiled cruelly. Now the game would begin.

The bell clanged. Santiago jumped up and winked at his cousin. It was the sign for him to throw the match. Chubs stared back at him with a determined expression. Santiago took that as a good sign and reached out for his cousin's beefy arm. Santiago pulled and tugged, but his cousin wouldn't budge. "Dammit man," he grunted under his breath. "Go down." Chubs still didn't move, so Santiago decided to elbow him in the ribs. It produced a heavy grunt.

Santiago grinned. He may not be strong, but he did have bony elbows.

Chubs didn't react at all. How was Santiago supposed to win if his cousin just stood there like a cow in the center of the road?

Santiago climbed up on the ropes to the steel post — like he'd seen his heroes do countless times before on TV. He was going to pin his cousin down once and for all, he thought, taking a deep breath as he crouched down. Santiago jumped, catapulting himself up into the air like a missile toward his opponent. But Chubs twirled quickly out of Santiago's path. With a loud thump, Santiago hit the floor. It felt like he'd broken every bone in his body. Chubs hopped onto Santiago and pinned him to the floor.

"What do you think you're doing?" Santiago grunted, squirming like a fish out of water. His ribs were getting crushed under his cousin's weight.

"Dude," his cousin hissed back. "El Payaso made me an offer."

"So what, man? The two of us had a deal. You lose. I win."

"But I don't want to lose," Chubs said, in a quiet voice. "I want to win. El Payaso said he'd give me five hundred dollars."

"What? Oh, hell no, man. We had a deal," Santiago hissed.

"Five hundred dollars!" Chubs exclaimed. "That's a lot of money. Do you know how much I can buy with five hundred dollars? I could finally buy a big van like I've always wanted."

"Chubs." Santiago's heart started to race at the gravity of the situation. He had to convince his cousin to get off him now! "Chubs, this is not about you. This is about the business. If you want I could give you seven hundred dollars — after we get rich. Besides you already have that sweet ride."

"It's my mom's."

"But she lets you drive it whenever you want."

The referee began to count out next to him.

"No!" Santiago cried, trying to squirm free. He was grateful for the olive oil he'd put on his arms and legs earlier. It made his skin greasy and gave him an extra inch of wiggle room. But his cousin dug down on his ribs with his elbows. The piercing pressure made his eyes bulge and his stomach want to hurl. Santiago felt tears sting his eyes. He could not let it end like this.

Then Chubs released a small chuckle. It was so soft, Santiago almost missed it. Was his cousin taunting him? He wondered as he slowly moved his fingers again over a tender spot along his cousin's torso. Chubs stiffened up. He gasped for breath, curling away from Santiago's fingertips, and laughed out loud. Santiago's eyes grew with understanding as he flexed his fingers and attacked him with tickle power.

"Stop! I give up!" Chubs cried, rolling into a ball.

The crowd jumped out of their seats. They were cheering at the top of their lungs. Santiago jumped onto his cousin, straddling him between his legs. Chubs shook under Santiago's weight. He tried to block Santiago's fingertips from reaching his ticklish spots. But his efforts were in vain. Santiago had a firm grip and he was not going to let go.

Santiago motioned to the referee to come over with the flick of his head. The balding man in the striped shirt stared at the scene. Never in all his years had he seen a *Lucha Libre* match won by tickling. The man glanced over his shoulder at Juan "El Payaso" Diamante. Santiago followed the referee's gaze. El Payaso was roaring with laughter and slapping his cowboy hat on his knee. Maria Elena sat next to him, her arms and legs crossed in a defiant manner and an angry scowl on her pretty face.

Santiago couldn't help but throw her a kiss. She flinched as if stung with a dart and ran to the closest exit. This seemed to amuse El Payaso and he laughed even louder.

The referee counted down. Chubs squirmed like a worm in the sunlight and Santiago held firm and tickled him some more. Suddenly, the bell clanged, the match was over, and he had won. The crowd was on fire. They were calling his name: "Puma! Puma!"

Santiago rushed over to his corner of the ring. Fabi and Milo cheered excitedly for him. He extended his hand out to Fabi. She blushed and passed the pitcher of Leafy Valley Mojo to him. He raised it over his head and the audience cheered even louder. Santiago had won the hearts of his new clients.

chapter 8

Santiago raised the volume to the Spanish pop song on his truck radio as they unloaded to set up the smoothie stand the next day. He was feeling great and shook his hips as he sang the chorus. Alexis joined him, waving bundled leafy greens in the air like pom-poms. Fabi couldn't stop laughing as she arranged the table. She was relieved Santiago had won the wrestling match. Now, they each waited in anticipation for the crowds of thirsty customers to appear. Grandpa Frank had stayed home, complaining of a bad back this morning. It was up to them to make this stand a success.

Alexis began to decorate the tables with curling branches and flowers she'd collected from the ranch while everyone else was loading the truck. She'd found a plastic floral tablecloth in the garage, and she spread it over the mixing station. Santiago liked it. It made the stand pop with color and the cloth hung down to the floor, creating an excellent hiding place for the food scraps.

Santiago glanced over at Fabi. She was busy arranging bunches of carrots in a wicker basket. "Well, at least this time Grandpa won't eat all the vegetables before the customers get here," she teased.

Suddenly, she cursed loudly. Santiago did a double take because he wasn't used to hearing her talk like that.

"What's the problem?" Santiago asked, not wanting anything to ruin his good day. They had a lot to do this morning. He had even woken up before dawn to get to *la pulga* before it opened in anticipation of all the new customers.

"We definitely have a thief here," Fabi cried, pointing to the empty basket of carrots. "A thief who likes to eat carrots."

Santiago raised the tablecloth and caught sight of a little boy's backside as he scurried away. In his hands dangled the purple carrots .

"I got this," Santiago hollered over his shoulder as he vaulted over the table. The table moaned under the pressure and another leg cracked, thrusting Santiago to the floor. "Dammit," Santiago cried. He couldn't hold back a small smile as he jumped up and patted his jeans clean.

"He's getting away," Fabi shouted, pointing up the aisle.

"I can help," Alexis volunteered.

"No," Santiago said. Alexis lowered her eyes. "I need you to stay here and help Fabi. Customers are going to be here any second. I'll be quick." He glanced down the aisle. "No one steals from El Puma," he cried, and turned to hunt down the carrot snatcher.

Santiago ran to the end of the walkway. People were filtering into *la pulga*. Families, couples, and mothers pushing strollers roamed up and down the row. He spun around quickly, worried that maybe he'd lost the kid. Suddenly, Santiago heard a commotion to his left. It sounded like an accident. A woman was yelling after a boy holding carrots. *That's him!* Santiago's eyes lit up. He took off behind a mound of used clothes and into the food court.

He caught sight of the carrot thief dodging customers like a crafty deer. A part of him admired the boy's agility. Santiago thought about turning back. If the boy wanted carrots badly enough to steal them, then maybe he deserved to have them. But then Santiago thought about his blossoming business. He couldn't afford to give up any more purple carrots. With this renewed resolve, Santiago increased his pace.

Suddenly, the boy stopped and turned back. Santiago ducked behind a red sofa, recognizing the boy. It was the kid from the wrestling match the night before. The little boy scanned the aisle behind him cautiously. Then he disappeared behind the restrooms.

Santiago crept around the concrete building slowly. He waited until he heard crisp crunching sounds. Then he jumped out screaming: "Aha! I caught you!"

However, the sight of two kids, even smaller than the thief, hungrily chomping at the carrots made him feel riddled with guilt. The kids jumped at the sound of Santiago's voice. They were about to run away when Santiago grabbed the thief by his jacket.

"Whoa, little man, where do you think you're going?"

He stared at Santiago, unable to speak or run. Santiago recognized their worry. It touched him in a strange way. They shouldn't be afraid of him, he thought. But then again, the boy did steal and stealing wasn't okay — he should know. "Is that my carrot?" he asked.

"No," the boy said in a hurried voice.

Santiago knew the kid was lying. Grandpa Frank was the only person in town who grew purple carrots. But how could he be mad at a kid who stole for his little siblings? He leaned down to the boy's eye level. "What's your name?"

"Angel."

"Isn't that a girl's name?" Santiago asked, laughing.

The boy frowned, "No. It's a boy's name. It's my dad's name."

Santiago quickly tried to recover. "Angel, all right. That's cool." He glanced back to the boy's siblings. They had to be only about three and four years old. The two little kids stared wide-eyed at him, still clutching their carrots.

"They call me Junior," he corrected.

Santiago nodded without listening. This little kid was a tough nut to crack, he thought. "You know stealing is not good. You're teaching your little brother and sister some bad habits."

"What do you know about bad habits?" the boy asked in a challenging voice. "You don't know us. I'm sorry about the carrots. I don't have any money." The boy emptied out his pockets. "You can call the cops if you want. I don't care." The boy crossed his arms in front of his chest.

"Whoa," Santiago said, raising his hands for him to calm down. "There's no need to get all testy, all right? You can have the carrots." He glanced at the younger kids crouched down against the back of the restroom. "Where's your mom?" he asked, turning to scan the area. She was the one who should be ashamed of herself. How could she let these little ones go hungry? That was just wrong.

The boy stared down at his red Converse and kicked at the dirt.

"Is she here?"

He shrugged his shoulders. Santiago didn't know what to think. He couldn't let these kids go hungry. So the boy stole some carrots from him? *Everyone has a right to food,* Santiago thought. He kneeled down to look at the boy eye to eye. "Next time, just ask and I can have you do some stuff around the booth in exchange for food."

"Really?" the boy asked, his face lighting up.

"Sure, little Angel." Santiago smiled, ruffling the kid's hair.

The kid frowned, but then he gave in to Santiago's charm and shrugged the name change off. He thanked Santiago and then ushered his little brother and sister away from the restroom.

Santiago waited a moment, watching the children walk away. The image pulled at his heart. He ached to do something, but he didn't know what. His mom would know what to do. She was a social worker. It was her job to help people. But he wasn't talking to his mom quite yet. Santiago decided to talk to Fabi, instead. She had good ideas about stuff like this.

He walked briskly back to his stand. It was probably out of control with customers fighting to place their orders right now. He smiled as he hurried down the path. However, when Santiago turned the corner to his row, he stopped dead in his tracks.

El Payaso's bodyguards were upturning crates and stomping vegetables on the floor of the stand. Alexis and Fabi were screaming for them to stop. They were each hanging from one of the first guy's arms like ornaments on a Christmas tree. But they were no match for the menacing men in black.

"What the hell are you doing?" Santiago cried, jumping in front of the other guy, trying to block him from further destruction.

The man told him in Spanish to move and without waiting for a response, shoved Santiago into the table, making the pyramid of oranges tumble to the floor.

"Stop!" Fabi called out, waving her arms in the air. "Please stop!" Tears streamed down her cheeks as she hurried to the ground and began to fill her T-shirt with oranges.

"Why are you doing this?" Santiago asked. They'd paid their fees. Why were they being harassed?

"Because I can," a familiar female voice said from behind him. For a split second, Santiago closed his eyes and prayed for someone to wake him from this horrible dream. But when he turned and looked upon Maria Elena's evil grin, he knew he was trapped in some sick payback game of hers. Her jeweled hands sparkled as they rested on her full hips. Santiago took in her styled hair, professional makeup, skimpy outfit, and platform heels. She looked like one of those glammed-up Bratz dolls — all plastic and no heart.

"Hey, baby." Santiago tried to make his voice honey-sweet. "I'm sorry if I upset you the other day. I really am. But don't you think this is going a bit too far?"

"Too far?" Maria Elena asked, her voice full of rage. "I wanted them to cut off your fingers but..." She stopped as if pricked. "Daddy wouldn't let me." The two bodyguards came to stand on either side of her like bookends. Maria Elena smiled. "I decided to destroy something you care about instead — your stupid little smoothie stand." She beamed triumphantly.

"That's not fair," Fabi said, picking up a squashed melon from the floor. It oozed fleshy juice onto her shirt. "We have a right to be here like everyone else."

Maria Elena started to laugh like a crazy person. It raised the hairs on the back of

Santiago's neck. "My daddy owns the land, but it's in my name, so technically I own it." She paused a moment to let her words sink in. "You" — she poked Santiago hard on the chest — "are a no-good, lying cheater. I don't want you or your stinking cousins, or your precious business at my *pulga*, you hear me?" Santiago stared in shock. "I'm going to make it so you never do business anywhere in Dos Rios ever again."

"You're insane," Santiago said, stepping away from Maria Elena. Her expensive perfume was making him dizzy.

"Well, this *pulga* sucks anyway," Alexis cut in, leaping ahead of Santiago. Fabi tried to pull Alexis back, but she shook her arm free. "And it doesn't even have a decent hair salon. The Brownsville *pulga* is so much better."

"Oh, yeah," Maria Elena said, stepping up to challenge Alexis. "That's pretty big talk for a girl who's about to get beat."

Santiago worried for Alexis. She wasn't strong like Fabi, who carried heavy plates of fajitas six days a week, nor was she mean like Maria Elena, who hired muscle to do her dirty work so she wouldn't break a nail.

"Ladies, stop," Santiago said, sliding in between them. "You win," he said to Maria Elena, "I'll leave." Fabi and Alexis protested behind him. Santiago motioned for them to be quiet. "You can have your stand. You can have your *pulga*. But you'll never have my love."

"What did you say?" Maria Elena's voice cracked as tears welled up in her eyes.

"You heard me," Santiago said. "I will never love you." He motioned to Fabi and Alexis to load up the truck. His cousins nodded in agreement and began to pile the remaining vegetables and fruits into crates. Santiago grabbed the blender in one arm and the tip jar in the other and walked over to his truck. Maria Elena called out to him.

"Come back here." Her voice shot up in alarm. "Santiago! I'm not done talking to you. Don't walk away from me. This is still my *pulga* and while you're on it, you have to do what I say. Santiago!"

Santiago didn't respond. He gathered fruit from the ground and tossed it into the flatbed as he tried to tune out Maria Elena's rant. There was a big hole in his heart, but it wasn't for Maria Elena. The smoothie stand was his baby. It pained him to see the torn piece of aloe on the ground. How could she have so little respect for food? he thought. Some people had nothing to eat. Little Angel stole to feed his siblings and this girl thought that this food, the stand, and his dreams were all a joke.

"You don't really mean that," Maria Elena said behind him. Anxiety filled her voice. "Santiago? Remember when you told me you thought I was the prettiest girl in the Valley?" She huffed loudly. "Fine. You can have your stand. I didn't mean for you to leave. I was just mad. But I'm not anymore. You can stay, okay? Santiago?"

Santiago continued to pack up and ignored her. Fabi and Alexis didn't wait around to see what Maria Elena would do next and jumped in the truck. Santiago started the engine just as Maria Elena began to scream "sorry" at the top of her lungs. She ran up to the driver's window and begged Santiago to stop and talk to her. When he wouldn't respond, Maria Elena turned to her goons and told them to do something. Santiago took off down the path and out of the Dos Rios *pulga*.

"Whoa," Alexis said, shaking herself. "That was crazy. Talk about a Llorona."

Fabi glanced sideways at her cousin. "You actually dated *her*?"

Santiago buried his hurt and put on a smile for Fabi. "I used to like the crazy ones." He shrugged.

"I think you should find yourself a boring girl, for a change."

"Yeah," Alexis teased. "One that has glasses and reads books."

Santiago forced himself to laugh as he turned at a light. He knew they meant well. But Maria Elena had killed his smoothie business. The full weight of what just happened hadn't quite hit him yet.

"Hey, what are we going to do with all the food?" Fabi asked. "We don't want it to go to waste." She crossed her arms in front of her chest, thinking. "I guess we could try and convince my dad to let us sell smoothies at the restaurant."

Alexis rolled her eyes. "Yeah right, like Dad's going to let you walk in and change the menu."

Suddenly, Santiago spotted a little boy walking away from the pulga with two smaller kids, hand-in-hand. He recognized the boy's red Converse and instantly knew what he wanted to do with all the food.

chapter 9

Santiago decided to take some time off. He needed to regroup and plan his next steps. The Leafy Valley Mojo was so close to taking off. Neighbors stopped him on the street to ask where they could pick up his mojo drink. The word was out. He just needed a location and money to set up his business on a more permanent basis.

He was on his way to his mother's house for dinner when his phone rang. It was Chubs. They hadn't talked since the wrestling match, so Santiago was a bit uneasy. Was his cousin still sore about losing? He answered on the third ring.

"Hey, bro, how's it going?"

"All right," Chubs replied. The silence that followed made Santiago nervous. Then his cousin said, "Yo, man, tickling should be grounds for disqualification."

Santiago relaxed. "Hey, I won fair and square. It's not my fault you're super-ticklish."

"Yeah, well, you owe me, bro."

"Dude, Maria Elena ran me out of *la pulga*. I lost my stand. Don't you think I've paid enough?"

"Yeah, but you still owe me. El Payaso was going to give me a lot of money if I won. I would have shared, you know."

Santiago waited expectantly for Chubs's request.

"I need you to do me a huge favor," Chubs said.

"What is it?"

"I need your truck tonight."

"What's wrong with the Mustang?"

Chubs hesitated. "Bro, I got in a fight with my mom. She's on my back about getting a job again. I got this opportunity that may prove very profitable, but I've got to make a delivery tonight. So what do you say?

Santiago understood his cousin's frustration. Chubs had dreams. He wanted to open a professional taxidermy shop. Like Santiago, Chubs needed money, so Santiago agreed to lend him his truck.

After lending his truck to Chubs, Santiago walked down the block toward his *tío's* restaurant. The sky had darkened and the streets were deserted. At night, parts of Dos Rios looked like a ghost town, especially with all the "For Sale" signs posted on building walls. The only blinking and beaming eyesore was the new Mr. Taco Man shop up ahead. Santiago was tempted to grab a late night snack, but his uncle's traditional restaurant was just across the street. Someone from his family would definitely spot him and that would be the end of him. Suddenly, a loud commotion made him come to a complete halt.

A noisy scuffle had erupted in front of the Mr. Taco Man store. A girl started to scream. Santiago felt his heart skip. He knew that voice. It was Fabi.

Santiago ran down the street. Fabi was struggling violently. Her dark hair shook wildly around the two men who held her arms down and pulled her down the sidewalk. Santiago feared the worst until he recognized the Taco Man uniforms and relaxed a bit. Behind her, Fabi's buddy Milo was also getting thrown out of the fast-food shop. Milo struggled a bit. In his hands were a bunch of flyers that he hastily threw to the ground. Santiago ran up to Fabi's assailants. He grabbed one of the guy's wrists and twisted it off her. He raised his fist in a threatening manner to the other guy.

"What the hell do you think you're doing?" Santiago cried to the Taco Man employees.

A tall young man in a business suit walked up to Santiago. He had a long straight nose and wore his hair neatly combed to the side. "Do you know this girl?" His voice was crisp and annoyed.

"Yeah, she's my *prima*. Who are you?" Santiago asked in a challenging voice.

"I'm the manager of Mr. Taco Man," the guy answered. "This little pest here has been sneaking around my business, scaring away customers and passing out flyers." He shoved an orange paper in Santiago's face that called for a Mr. Taco Man boycott and support for local small business. A small smile crept on Santiago's face and he glanced at his cousin.

Fabi struggled free from the taco men. "You should all be ashamed of yourselves. Do you even know what you're doing to Dos Rios? Small businesses can't compete with your big-chain money. Look around. You're turning our community into a ghost town."

The manager threw his hands up in the air. "Get that girl out of here right now or I'm calling the cops! You hear me?"

Fabi was on a rampage and wasn't going to be intimidated. "Oh, and I found out what's in the 'secret' sauce, amigo! High-fructose corn syrup, MSG, and a bunch of chemical preservatives I can't even pronounce! The people won't stand for this! They won't. People will rise up and shut you down, Mr. Taco Manager!"

"No one is forcing our customers to eat anything," the manager snapped back. He noticed the small crowd that had gathered around them and gave a nervous snort as he fixed his tie. "I'll let this go because I'm a good person. I'm just a simple businessman trying to feed my family and provide jobs in the Valley," he said to the crowd. The crowd murmured around them.

"You're destroying our community!" Fabi spat.

It was time to rein Fabi in, Santiago thought. He grabbed his cousin and Milo by the arms and pulled them both across the street. Through the windows of his uncle's restaurant, Santiago recognized the entire family watching the scene unfold.

"I don't want to see that girl around here ever again!" the man yelled as his workers ushered their customers back into the eatery. "I've got her on tape, you know. I'll sue your whole family for defamation!"

Santiago pushed Fabi through the front door of the restaurant, ignoring her complaints. Once inside, the room erupted in forceful outbursts and questions. Fabi slumped into a chair, grumbling under her breath—Milo followed. Santiago grabbed a chair and twirled it backward and sat across from them. The rest of the family huddled behind him, waiting for an explanation.

"Fabi, Milo," Santiago pressed in a serious voice. "What the hell were you two thinking?" His question set off a stream of voices behind him. Santiago glanced over his shoulder at the faces of his *tío* Leo, *tía* Magda, grandma Trini, *abuelita* Alpha, grandpa Frank, and even Alexis, all yelling on top of one another. Fabi slumped back in her chair, frowning.

"Guys," Santiago turned to address the group behind him. "One at a time, all right?" The group settled down.

Fabi took a deep breath. "Well, you know how we were spying on Mr. Taco Man?" Her mother objected, but Abuelita Alpha told her to let Fabiola explain.

Fabi continued. "We" — she gestured at Milo — "decided to pretend to apply for positions there." There were whispers behind him, but Santiago tuned them out and focused on what Fabi said next. "I got a look at the kitchen and their pantry. I couldn't believe all the chemicals they use in the food."

"And that's when we decided to do something about it," Milo cut in. Fabi shot Milo a grateful smile as he continued. "We went online and looked up what the ingredients were and we found all this stuff about what preservatives and pesticide toxins do to the body and we felt like we had to let people know."

"You had no right to go over there and start trouble," Fabi's father said in an angry voice. "Don't you ever think with that thick skull of yours? He threatened to sue us. We can't have that. We'll lose the restaurant for sure and then what are we all supposed to do, eat dirt?"

"She was just trying to help," Alexis cried from the back. *Tío* Leo ignored the interruption.

"But, Dad," Fabi interrupted, "we have to do something. They're stealing our customer base. Business has dropped since they opened a couple weeks ago. I even saw your buddies" — she looked up at Grandpa Frank — "Cherrio and Chepe eating the Mucho Macho Taco fiesta pie. That's when I kind of lost it." Fabi looked over her shoulder out the window, anger flashing across her face. "I couldn't believe that they would betray us like that."

"No one is betraying anyone," *Tío* Leo said in a tired voice. Fabi looked up at her dad in surprise. "You complain that Mr. Taco Man is unhealthy. But you also complain about our menu, too."

Fabi flinched and her cheeks reddened.

"*Mija*, I know you're trying to help. But people can eat whatever and wherever they want. That man was right about that. No one is forcing them to eat there. Four tacos for a dollar, I can't compete with that. But for some people that meal will make sure their family doesn't go to bed hungry. We all have to make a living. We all need to eat. Times are tough and there are few jobs outside of fast-food joints around town." He sighed. "I know your frustration, *mija*. I remember when downtown was the place to be on a Saturday night." His eyes lit up as he remembered. He turned back to Fabi and the light had dimmed. "Do you think this is the first business that's ever opened up across the street from us?" Fabi didn't know how to answer. She glanced at Milo and then at Santiago.

"But, Dad," Fabi tried again, "I don't want fajitas that come from some California warehouse. I want 'Made in the Rio Grande Valley' tortillas. I want to support the people who live and struggle here. Just because things have changed doesn't mean we have to roll over and accept it. The few businesses left can stand together. We have to fight to save our community. If we do nothing, there will be no family businesses left."

Leo leaned back in his chair. He said nothing and stared off into his kitchen. Then his big brown face relaxed into an easy smile. Leo chuckled. "I don't know when you became such an activist, *mija*."

Fabi beamed, tears rolling down her face. "I don't know, either, Dad, but this is something

I care about." Leo jumped up and gave his daughter a hug.

"And we can offer something Mr. Taco Man can never sell," Santiago interrupted. Everyone turned to gaze at him. "Leafy Valley Mojo, baby. Made with the best local vegetables and fruits the Rio Grande Valley can provide."

Tío Leo laughed and slapped Santiago on the back. "Okay, Santiago," he said, "we'll try out your smoothie stand up front on one condition."

"Anything."

"That you make sure Fabiola works on those recipes until they actually taste good."

The room erupted into bursts of laughter. Fabi cried, "Not funny!" from the opposite side of the room. Santiago grinned. He felt relieved and happy that everything was working out. Fabi was talking with enthusiasm to Grandma Trini and her mother. She was planning a meeting with the entire neighborhood. They would hold it at the restaurant and invite local business owners, the city council members, and anyone who cared about preserving the local economy. Santiago crossed his arms across his chest and grinned.

A pulsing vibration in his back pocket surprised him. His cousin Chubs was calling him. Santiago hoped his cousin hadn't gotten into an accident.

"Yo, what's up?" he asked, putting one hand over his ear so he could hear.

"Bro, thank God you answered," Chubs cried in an anxious voice. "Dude, I messed up big-time. The Salinas brothers are going to kill me."

chapter 10

Dude," Chubs cried anxiously into the phone. "I was totally robbed by this wino. He stole your truck and now I'm here with a bunch of rotting fruit on the side of the road. Pick me up, man."

Santiago's eyes widened with fury. Then his phone beeped again. He was getting another call. It was his mom. "Hold up a second," Santiago told his cousin as he switched the line over. "Mom. What's up?"

"You said you were coming home tonight," his mother reminded, trying to sound patient, but he could hear bubbling tension in her voice.

"Yeah, I was on my way, but —"

"Great, I'll see you in ten minutes. We need to talk," she said before hanging up.

Santiago groaned, looking at the cell phone screen that blinked, indicating his cousin still on hold. He clicked to Chubs. "Bro . . . I . . . errrr. I need to stop by the house for a second and then —"

"Oh, hell naw!" his cousin complained. "You going to just leave me out here with the wild animals?"

"What animals? Where you at?"

"I'm like ten miles outside of the Laguna Ovalle Reserve. You remember where that is?"

Santiago remembered vividly the wildlife refuge where they used to go as kids to explore the clay dunes, watch falcons, and try to catch the endangered ocelots. "What are you doing all the way out there at this time of night? You told me you were going to make a delivery, that's it. I should call your mom to go get you."

"No!" Chubs cried. "Santiago, I know I messed up. I'm sorry, man. But nobody can know where I'm at. My mom would kill me double if she found out I was working for the Salinas brothers." Santiago nodded. Although Chubs was nineteen, he still lived with his mother and feared her more than the Salinas brothers.

"Fine. Hang tight. I'll be there as soon as I can," Santiago said, releasing his breath. "But I need to find a car first."

"Well, hurry up, man. It's cold out here."

Santiago was about to tell him off, but held his tongue. His cousin was hopeless. Now, he'd gotten the truck stolen! Santiago wanted to hit something. His family was buzzing with excitement around him, but Santiago was a hundred miles away. He hung up the phone and asked his grandmother for a ride to his mother's house. On the way, he wondered about the trouble Chubs was dragging him into. Dread filled every inch of his body. The Salinas brothers hadn't bothered Santiago, ever since he promised Juan "El Payaso" Diamante to stay out of any illegal activities. He wondered if El Payaso had told the brothers something. But now his cousin was in trouble and his own truck was in the middle of it!

An unfamiliar car was parked in his mother's driveway when he arrived. Santiago hurried up to the house and let himself in.

"Hey, Mom," he called out from the door. "I'm home."

"In the kitchen," his mother replied. He smelled something good cooking. Did they have company?

Santiago found his mother serving his father a bowl of spaghetti with meatballs. The scene made his stomach turn. What was he doing here?

"Hey, Mom, I have to go now," Santiago said, ignoring his father. "Can I borrow your car?"

"Santiago." His mother's face dropped. "I

[155]

was hoping we could all sit and talk about your future. What's wrong with your truck?"

"Mom, I can't talk about it now. Chubs took my truck and now he needs my help."

"Help? Did he run out of gas?" his father volunteered.

Santiago's eyes widened. "No, it's cool. I got this. Mom? Your car?" He extended his hand.

"Oh, c'mon, don't be like that," his father said in a playful voice. "If he's in a jam, you might need me — plus I have a full tank of gas."

Santiago frowned at his mother. Why wasn't she saying anything? He bit his lip, glancing from his mother to his father. But this was not a game. Chubs was in way over his head and the Salinas brothers didn't give second chances.

His father stared, waiting for an answer. Finally, Santiago let out a deep breath. He didn't want his father to think he had forgiven him — not by a long shot. But he also couldn't overlook his dad's past criminal experience. It might be just what they needed.

His mother walked over to him. "Santiago, I don't know what your cousin has gotten himself into, but I'd feel a lot better if your father was there."

"Fine," Santiago said, surrendering. He turned to leave. "Let's go." He didn't even check to see if his father was following him. Santiago was trying to stay cool even though a small part of him was relieved that he would not be going after Chubs alone.

"Do you want to drive?" his father asked, jingling the keys in front of Santiago.

"Whatever. I don't care. I only agreed to you coming along because Chubs has my truck and I don't want my mom to worry," Santiago spat angrily.

"Yo," his dad said. "I just thought you might want to drive. That's all."

It was a nice gesture, but Santiago didn't want him to think they were friends now. "Okay. Thanks."

• • •

The drive to Laguna Ovalle felt like the longest ride of Santiago's life. His father kept trying to start a conversation with him. He asked about school; if he had any serious girlfriends; what he liked to do for fun. Santiago dodged his questions like they were poisonous darts. He turned on the radio to drown out any hope of a father-son bonding session. His father turned off the radio.

"Dammit, Santiago, I'm trying to talk to you," he said. Santiago pressed down on the accelerator, frowning at the road ahead of him. "Okay, so you don't want to talk to me," his dad continued. "I get that. But there's something I've been meaning to tell you."

Santiago couldn't help but sigh. Why did every adult feel the need to talk to him?

"You know, your moms and I talked. I know I haven't been around much . . . but I'm here now. Your mom told me about you dropping out of school and I just wanted you to know that I think that's a bad decision."

Santiago pulled off the road and slammed on the brakes. He couldn't believe his ears. This man was giving him advice! "Stop!" Santiago cried. "Stop trying to act like you care! Stop trying to wiggle your way back into our family! It's not going to happen!" Santiago looked at his father. All he could feel was pain and frustration boiling up inside him. "You know the day the cops busted you, I was glad. It meant that I didn't have to see Mom get beat up anymore. It meant I could have a normal life and I didn't have to cry myself to sleep." Santiago felt the heat rise to his face and his eyes sting with tears, but he pushed on. "You were never there for us, even when you were around. You never came to my Little League games or took me hunting like dads are supposed to. And now you want me to forget about all that and welcome you into my life with open arms. It's never going to happen." There was a long uncomfortable pause between them. His father slouched down in his seat.

"I appreciate you coming with me and all. But after tonight, you can just get lost!" Santiago said, putting the car into gear. They drove on for another thirty minutes in silence.

They found Chubs sitting on the ground on the side of the highway. He rushed over to the vehicle out of breath.

"Oh, man, I'm so glad to see you. I was worried you were going to leave me out here." Chubs noticed Santiago's father. "Hey, *tío* Eddy. Is that you? No way! You look exactly the same. It's so good to see you —" He cut himself off and shot Santiago an uneasy glance.

"Just get into the car," Santiago said, gesturing for Chubs to hurry up. "We need to find my truck."

Chubs squeezed into the front seat, pushing Eddy right up next to Santiago. He could smell his dad's cologne. It brought back childhood images of playing dress-up in his dad's clothes. Santiago pushed those memories down and inched away. The man's closeness made him uncomfortable.

"Yeah," Chubs nodded, excitedly. "Let's catch that punk. Catch him before it's too late."

"So, what's this all about?" Eddy asked, turning to Chubs.

His cousin's cheeks reddened. "*Tío*, well, you remember how I liked to do taxidermy? Well, the Salinas brothers thought it would be clever to hide some stuff inside the animals." Chubs looked from Santiago to Eddy for a reaction. "I did it and they came out real nice. I'm supposed to deliver them tonight. I was on my way when I saw this tore-up dude selling fruit and vegetables on the side of the road. I thought it was kind of strange because we're way out in the country. But the guy was from Dos Rios. He was real wasted and he was crying about his three hungry kids at home and how he had no money. I felt bad for him. Then I thought about your business, Santiago." His cousin's voice brightened. "And how you could use the fruits to make that green juice. So I offered to buy everything from him. I got out to help him load the truck when that jerk jumped in and took off with all my stuffed animals." Chubs became very quiet. "Now the Salinas brothers are going to kill me because I lost their merchandise."

"You left the keys in the ignition!" Santiago cried, trying to see over his dad. "You deserve whatever you get for being so stupid."

Chubs lowered his head. "I know. I know." He sighed, feeling the weight of the situation on his shoulders.

"Wait a second," Eddy cut in. "Maybe we can find this guy before the Salinas brothers notice their stuff is missing." Santiago turned to his father in surprise.

"Really, *tío*?" Chubs asked, wide-eyed.

"But I want the two of you to make me a promise," Eddy said, growing serious.

"Yes!" Chubs exclaimed before Santiago could object.

"I want you boys to go back to school —
you have to finish high school."

Santiago felt like the frame of the car was
coming down on him. Why did everything have
to go back to school? Was this his mother's
meddling?

"We'll do it!" Chubs answered for both
of them.

"I'll think about it," Santiago muttered.

Eddy smiled brightly. "All right, that's good
enough for me. The way I see it, there are only
two possibilities. The wino is either going to
try and sell the truck to score some booze or
he's out for a joyride."

Chubs frowned. "He could be anywhere by
now. He has a three-hour head start. Man, he
could be deep in Mexico for all I know."

Eddy pulled his cell phone from his shirt
pocket. "It's a good thing I have a lot of friends,"
he said, before making a few calls. Santiago
turned on the car and headed back to Dos Rios.
A small smile crept over Santiago's lips. His

[163]

father's quick thinking and resourcefulness were impressive.

It took them most of the night to track down Santiago's truck. The car thief had tried to sell it at two used-car lots and even to a wrecking company outside the town of Zapata.

Twenty miles east of the wrecking company they spotted a man with scraggly hair and stained jeans pushing a black truck with a blue tarp spread out over the back. Santiago pulled over to the shoulder and got out.

"Need some help there?" his father asked the man, surprising Santiago. He hadn't even heard his dad get out of the car.

The car thief glanced over his shoulder and smiled sheepishly. He was missing his two front teeth. "Yeah, I guess I ran out of gas," the man said. "You mind giving me a lift to a gas station?"

"That's a fine looking truck you have there," Eddy said, coming up beside him.

"You like it? I'll sell it to you for a real good price." The man noticed Santiago. "Is that your son? I have a son, too. He's a good boy, but he grows so fast. See this —" He pulled out a pair of red Converse from inside the truck. "Don't fit him no more. That's why I need to sell the truck. To buy him some new shoes." He looked at Santiago. "You want to buy some shoes? They're almost like new. Hey, you guys got any beer?"

Santiago recognized the red Converse. Those were Angel's shoes. How did this wino get Angel's shoes? Then it all clicked into place. This was Angel's dad! A memory flashed before his eyes. He remembered waiting for his dad on the first day of school. He turned down a ride from his kindergarten teacher, because he knew his dad wouldn't forget him. His dad never came. And there were countless other times Santiago made excuses for his dad's absence. His dad, like Angel's dad, didn't deserve to be called "father." A flare of anger ignited in his chest.

Santiago tackled the man to the ground. He grabbed the man by his soiled collar and shook him violently. Tears streamed down Santiago's face and he socked the man in the mouth with all his strength. He couldn't stop himself. He couldn't think. Strong arms pulled him away. Santiago kicked and screamed: "What's wrong with you? Why can't you be a dad?"

Angel's dad stared at Santiago from behind a busted lip and a bloody nose. He curled into a ball and cried: "*¡Mi hijo!*"

Chubs leaned over Santiago and asked, "Bro, are you all right?"

Santiago nodded. His pulse was thumping out of control. Eddy stood off to the side watching the scene. He lit a cigarette.

Chubs released Santiago and rushed over to grab the keys from the truck. Then he waved them at Santiago triumphantly. The man on the ground tried to protest. But Chubs growled at him to stay down. Chubs looked under the blue tarp, checking to make sure his cargo was still there. Santiago noticed his cousin relax. Then his cousin raised one of his crazy stuffed owls with antlers over his head. Chubs ripped off the head of the owl and looked inside. *Idiot*, Santiago thought, shaking his head. Maybe they should go back to school! They were certainly no good at smuggling or wrestling. Maybe he could study business? Santiago liked the sound of that. He was about to tell his cousin about his new idea when he heard the sound of police sirens coming in their direction. His blood turned cold.

"Get in the car," Eddy yelled. "The guy at the wrecking company must have called the cops!"

Chubs reached for the stuffed animals, but his arms could only carry so many and the sirens were getting closer. Santiago yelled at his cousin to leave it behind.

"But the Salinas brothers. They're expecting their delivery. And your truck —" Chubs caught himself in midsentence.

Santiago felt his heart leap into his throat. His truck! The drugs! How would he explain this? He looked from the truck to his dad. The wino was lying on the ground, looking up into the sky — totally oblivious to the situation. Maybe he could get Angel's dad back into the truck. He could say that the truck was stolen. But what about the animals stuffed with drugs? Santiago grunted loudly, pulling at his hair. This was so unfair. His smoothie stand was about to take off and he was even thinking of going back to school.

Santiago looked back down at the wino. Could he let Angel's dad take the blame? What was worse: a bad dad or no dad? Santiago couldn't think. He didn't want to make this decision. Against his better judgment, he went back and helped Angel's dad up off the ground. He didn't know how he would explain this situation to the cops, but he wouldn't be the reason Angel grew up without a dad.

"What are you doing?" Chubs cried.

"I can't just leave him to take the rap," Santiago shouted back.

"Why not? Let the fool take the blame. He's already costing me a couple thousand, not to mention what the Salinas brothers will do to me when they find out," Chubs cried. "Plus he smells."

"His son is my friend," Santiago explained. He pushed the man in the backseat of his dad's car. Then Santiago turned to search for his dad. The sirens were almost on them. Eddy was standing in the same spot. He kicked a rock and walked slowly toward the truck. "Hey, what are you doing?" Santiago called out to him. "Let's get out of here."

His father turned. His eyes were sad. "Someone has to take the blame."

Santiago shook as if waking from a nightmare. "What? No. Wait. We can leave the wino. We can say he stole the car."

Eddy smiled softly. "He stole a truck full of drugs that's in my son's name." He shook his head. "It's better I take this one for the team. I don't want you boys to get in trouble anymore." He walked up to Santiago and reached out and squeezed his shoulder. "That's what I was trying to tell you earlier."

"But, Dad." Santiago's voice cracked on the word "Dad." "You just got out. It's not fair."

Eddy made a sour face as if he was having a hard time trying to control his emotions. "Promise me you'll write," Eddy said, his eyes growing misty.

"Dad, don't do this," Santiago cried.

Chubs grabbed Santiago from behind and pulled him toward the car. "We got to go now."

"Please, Dad," Santiago called out. "Dad! Don't do this."

Eddy motioned for them to get going. Chubs pushed Santiago into the car and slammed the door behind him. Then he rushed to the driver's seat and started the car. They drove away from the scene. Santiago turned back, tears welling up in his eyes. Eddy stood in the middle of the street. He raised his right arm to wave good-bye. Suddenly, red and blue lights appeared from the distance. Eddy Reyes turned toward the blaring sirens to meet the police officers.

chapter 11

Santiago felt a deep ache inside of him. He reached for his chest, wondering if this is what a heart attack felt like.

"Are you okay, bro?" Chubs asked, glancing sideways.

Santiago rubbed at the pain in this chest. "Yeah, I guess I'm just tripping out."

"I know, huh?" Chubs agreed. "I don't even know how I'm going to begin to explain this to the Salinas brothers."

Santiago just shrugged. "We'll tell them the truth. We'll say that we were on our way to make the delivery when we got pulled over by the cops. And that my pops took the blame."

Chubs stared blankly at the empty countryside before them. "I guess that's the end of my drug smuggling–taxidermy career. No one is going to want my services now after this bust. The cops will be on alert for any unusually stuffed animals."

Santiago couldn't help but laugh at his cousin's observation. Thanks to his father, they were spared a life of hard time.

"I owe your dad big-time," Chubs said in a serious voice. "I don't know how I'll ever repay him."

"I do."

"You do?" Chubs asked, surprised. "How?"

"Go back to school."

Chubs groaned, "Aw man, do we have to? I hate school. Teachers and tests and waking up early. Hey, aren't I too old? There's like a age limit, right?"

Santiago smiled and then glanced back at

Angel's dad in the backseat. His cousin followed his gaze.

"What are we going to do with Smelly over here?" Chub's asked.

"Let's get him home," Santiago said, pausing just a moment. Then he addressed the wino in the backseat: "Did you see what my dad just did? He sacrificed his freedom for us. That's what dads do. They make sure their kids have enough to eat and shoes on their feet. He may not be the best dad in the world" — Santiago felt a pang — "but he tried to do right by me back there." Santiago paused to let the words seep in. "We're not turning you over to the cops, because I know your son Angel. He's my friend. And he deserves a dad, too. So think of this as your second chance." The wino nodded. Frustrated, Santiago peered out the window into the dark brush landscape. He didn't know if the wino would change. But Santiago had to give Angel the chance he never got. Santiago sighed, his emotions twisting and pressing down on his chest like the constrictive embrace of a boa right before death.

A patrol car with flashing blue and red lights was parked in front of the house Angel's dad had given them directions to. Chubs stopped Eddy's car a safe distance away. They all began to panic. Did the authorities know about their involvement? Were they in the process of rounding everyone up for questioning? Angel's dad shook his head, refusing to get out, and dug his feet into the floor.

"Maybe we should just lie low a bit?" Chubs suggested, turning off the headlights.

Santiago lowered his window to try and hear what was going on. It could be a routine check-in. Maybe Angel's father was wanted for something else? Or maybe it had to do with the kids? A fit of anger seized him and Santiago pushed open the door and got out. Santiago grabbed Angel's dad by the shirt and pulled him out of his dad's car.

"You go see what's going on!" Santiago demanded. "Your kids could be hurt."

The man toppled down on the ground and curled up into a ball to either protect himself or stay put. Santiago wanted to kick him, but then he heard a bone-chilling cry that made him stiffen with fear.

"*Ay, mis hijos. Mis hijos,*" the pained female voice cried into the whistling wind. "*¿Dónde están mis hijos?*"

Santiago and Chubs glanced at each other, thinking the same thing: *La Llorona!* The heart-wrenching howls of a grieving mother were carried swiftly in the breeze and seemed to be coming from every direction. Chubs jumped out of the car and ran over to Santiago.

"Dude, did you hear that? It's *La Llorona*. It's really her. Wait till I tell Grandpa Frank!"

Santiago scanned the area. Something wasn't right. People were coming out of their homes, in their nightclothes, to see what was going on. Officers helped a bony woman wearing nothing but a white T-shirt down the front stairs. She was barefoot and her hair was sticking out in all angles like she hadn't combed it in weeks. This had to be Angel's mom, he thought. Santiago ran over to the house, not caring if they arrested him. The only thing he could think about was whether or not the kids were safe.

Then he saw his own mother walk out of Angel's house. Consuelo locked eyes with him for a moment. She motioned for him to follow her to her parked car.

Santiago's heart was racing. "Mom, where's Angel?"

"Where have you been? You were supposed to just pick up your cousin and come straight home. Your *tía* Bea and I have been up all night worrying about you two. You boys don't have the decency —" She stopped in midsentence. "Wait, what are you doing here?"

"Mom. I know these kids. Where's Angel?"

She sighed. "A neighbor called the cops. She heard the kids crying and came over to see what was going on. Those poor kids were starving. There was no food in the house and the mom was passed out on the floor. It was a good thing the neighbor came over when she did."

Santiago looked back for Angel's dad. His cousin was walking toward them. There was a dark look on his face. Santiago didn't have to ask, he already knew. Angel's dad was gone.

epilogue

The first-period bell rang at Dos Rios High School. Students rushed for their classrooms, anxious to not be marked tardy. As the hallway cleared, a lone figure stood defiantly behind, at the entrance. His sneakers stayed planted on the colorful mosaic of the school emblem: two fighting catfish. Santiago combed his fingers through his curly locks and walked to the assistant principal's office.

When Santiago entered the main office, Sylvia, the school secretary, let out a small cry.

She moved to call the principal or maybe school security, but Santiago motioned for her not to worry.

"The assistant principal has been expecting me," he said with great authority. Santiago walked up to the assistant principal's door and opened it.

John Castillo was struggling over a grant request to help pay for travel expenses for the school Mariachi Club. He hated to be interrupted and lashed out. "What is wrong with you? Can't you knock before entering?"

Santiago chuckled. "I guess there's some things you still got to teach me, huh, Castillo?"

Castillo jerked upright, not believing his eyes. "What are you doing here, Santiago?"

Santiago took a seat across from Castillo's desk and put his feet up on it. "Isn't it obvious? I'm trying to get an education. That's if you'll still have me."

Castillo came around his big desk and took a seat next to Santiago. "But what about your big plans? Your business? And that stuff about being a man and making real money?"

Santiago took a moment to take in the room: the messy desk, framed diplomas, and photograph of the Mariachi Club. His heart softened at the sight of his bandmates. Santiago shrugged. "I don't know what the hurry is with you grown-ups. Life is short and I've decided that I want to enjoy my last couple of months in high school. You know, go to football games, play in mariachi regional competitions, and go to my senior prom."

Castillo shook his head in amusement.

"Plus Rio Smoothie, my new and improved business, is going great. Last weekend, we had a line around the block."

"I know," Castillo said. "I was in it."

Santiago felt himself blush and lowered his voice. "I also have this little dude, he's like my little brother now. He comes and helps at the stand on the weekends and all. I want to be a good role model, you know? And well — my dad. I made him a promise and I want to keep it." Santiago looked up. "Please, Castillo, can I come back to school?"

The assistant principal leaned back in his chair and crossed his legs. He wanted to believe that Santiago had changed. He really did. He wasn't convinced, but Santiago's mother, Consuelo, would never forgive him if he didn't give her knucklehead son another chance.

"Well, it just so happens that we have an opening in the Mariachi Club."

Santiago's eyes lit up. He jumped up and gave Castillo a hug. "You won't regret it. It'll be just like old times. Oh, check this out. I've been thinking that the group should liven up its sound. You know, add a little hip-hop fusion mix. Or we can get some dancers in short mariachi miniskirts. Wouldn't that be hot?"

The assistant principal stared as Santiago rambled on and on. Castillo smiled. He was reminded of his mother's favorite saying, "*Caras vemos, corazones no sabemos.*"

acknowledgments

Muchísimas thank-yous to my fabulous cousins Carlos, Beto, Frankie, and Rickie, and my brother Kiki, for sharing your teenage *aventuras* and answering my gazillion questions. To Maria Elena and Juan Ovalle, *gracias* for your *chisme*, fact checking, and for being the best RGV consultants in the world. To the students of Brown Middle School and Tabitha Brocha, thanks for all your suggestions and ideas. To Frank Ramirez, Maclovia, and Eloy Sanchez, *gracias* for taking me into your families and sharing your experiences and knowledge *conmigo*. To Moses and Cynthia, *gracias* for taking me to the Weslaco *pulga*. To Sarah Cuadra and the whole Cuadra clan at Storybook Garden, thank you for sharing issues of small businesses and your sewing skills. To my niece, Jelly Moncada, thank you for reading the early drafts of this manuscript. To MaElena Igram, *gracias* for driving around the Valle and taking me to Zapata for the best chicken-fried steak. To my fabulous Star County tour guide Elizabeth Munoz, thank you for sharing your friends *y cuentos conmigo*. To *mi familia* and Marina Luna Suarez, *gracias por todo tu apoyo*. To Anna Bloom and the editorial team at Scholastic, *gracias* for your keen eyes, guidance, and making me look good. And to my biggest cheerleader and friend, Stefanie von Borstel, thank you for reading all my drafts, standing by me through tough cuts, and for always believing in me.

[When you live on the border, you have to follow the rules.]

border
town
Crossing the Line

MALÍN ALEGRÍA

"Oh, c'mon," Alexis protested, trying to twist out of her sister's grip. "This is high school, Fabi. I want to have fun. Do crazy things."

"You *will* do crazy things," Fabi said. "I promise. But trust me on this: You don't want to do them with Dex."

Alexis's eyes lit up. "That's his name? Dex. Dex what?"

"Dex Nada, because that boy is *nada* to you. Listen," Fabi said with a sigh. "Look, you've just got to trust me on this one. I'll explain at lunch, okay?" Then she hurried away to her own classroom on the second floor.

The Border Town drama continues in *Quince Clash.*

Melodee began to laugh, but then stopped. She stared Fabi in the eye, as if trying to drill a hole to the truth. "All right," she said with a nod. "You think your quince will be better than mine? It's on. You and me." She pointed to Fabi. "We'll have a quinceañera competition. And everyone here will vote."

Fabi felt the blood drain from her face. She never wanted a quinceañera in the first place. Now she had to have one—and not just any quinceañera. Fabi had to have the biggest, best quince the Valley had ever seen.